The Edge of When

Published in Canada by Fitzhenry & Whiteside, 195 Allstate Parkway, Markham, Ontario L3R 4T8

Published in the United States by Fitzhenry & Whiteside, 311 Washington Street, Brighton, Massachusetts
02135

www.fitzhenry.ca godwit@fitzhenry.ca

10 9 8 7 6 5 4 3 2 1

Library and Archives Canada Cataloguing in Publication
Matas, Carol, 1949-
The edge of when / Carol Matas.
It's up to us (originally publ. as The fusion factor), Zanu and Me,
myself and I first published: Saskatoon : Fifth House, 1986,
1986 and 1987 as part of Fifth perception series.
Re-issued: Toronto : General Paperback, 1991 as part of
Timetracks series.
Contents: It's up to us -- Zanu -- Me, myself and I.
ISBN 978-1-55455-198-9
I. Title. II. Title: Fusion factor. III. Title: It's up to us.
IV. Title: Zanu. V. Me, myself and I.
PS8576.A7994E45 2011   jC813'.54   C2011-901399-1

Publisher Cataloging-in-Publication Data (U.S)
Matas, Carol, 1949-
The edge of when / Carol Matas.
Originally published: Markham, ON: Fifth House Publishers, 1987.
[280] p. : cm.
Summary: Rebecca worries about the things a normal twelve-year-old girl would worry about: starting junior
high, her friends, her family. But when she witnesses a kidnapping and finds herself transported into a ter-
rifying world of the future, Rebecca not only must find her way home, she must figure out a way to alter the
course of history.
ISBN: 978-1-55455-198-9 (pbk.)
1. Time travel – Juvenile fiction. I. Title.
[F] dc22   PZ7.M423964Ed   2011

Fitzhenry & Whiteside acknowledges with thanks the Canada Council for the Arts, and the Ontario Arts
Council for their support of our publishing program. We acknowledge the financial support of the Government of Canada through the Canada Book Fund (CBF) for our publishing activities.

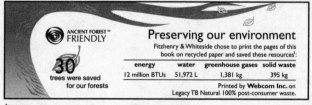

ANCIENT FOREST™ FRIENDLY

Preserving our environment
Fitzhenry & Whiteside chose to print the pages of this
book on recycled paper and saved these resources[1]:

energy	water	greenhouse gases	solid waste
12 million BTUs	51,972 L	1,381 kg	395 kg

30 trees were saved for our forests

Printed by **Webcom Inc.** on
Legacy TB Natural 100% post-consumer waste.

[1]Estimates were made using the Environmental Defense Paper Calculator.

FSC
www.fsc.org
MIX
Paper from
responsible sources
FSC® C004071

Cover design by Daniel Choi
Cover image courtesy of iStockphoto
Interior design by Comm Tech Unlimited
Printed in Canada

The Edge of When

CAROL MATAS

Fitzhenry & Whiteside

To:

My daughter, Rebecca,

My son, Sam,

My nephews, Michael, Jesse, Mark, and Eli

With love

Again.

C.M.

Dear Reader,

It was over thirty years ago that I published three books about a twelve-year-old girl from Winnipeg, Rebecca Lepidus. Rebecca was a time traveler and she encountered three different futures in the novels *The Fusion Factor*, *Zanu*, and *Me, Myself, and I*.

When my publisher informed me that these books were to be reprinted, I suggested we update them. Little did I realize what I was getting myself into! Not only have I updated the books, but I have merged them into one novel—cutting, changing, rewriting, and hopefully improving the whole.

Thirty years ago, the issues I was writing about seemed to me to be things that might happen in a far distant future—a nuclear catastrophe, a corporate takeover of democracy, climate change, rampant consumerism. Unfortunately, the themes of these books seem more urgent and relevant now than they did then.

So I hope, dear reader, as with all my books, you will enjoy *The Edge of When* as a good read and a thrilling adventure that you can't put down. I also hope that the subject matter will give you something to mull over. *What kind of future do we want? And what can each of us do to shape it?*

Yours,

Carol Matas

PART ONE

CHAPTER ONE

"Lonney!" screamed Rebecca at the top of her lungs. "*Lonne-e-e-y!*"

Rebecca stood at the top of the school steps.

"Wait, Lonney!" she screamed again as she leapt down the steps three at a time. Lonney was already halfway across the schoolyard, heading toward Fleet Street. "Wait up, Lonney Donnen, or you'll be sorry!"

As Rebecca raced across the schoolyard, Lonney sauntered along seemingly unaware of the shouting going on behind him. She caught up to him just as he entered the children's playground, which lay between the schoolyard and Fleet Street. He continued to walk.

Rebecca sprinted ahead a few feet then turned, blocking his way. She was hot and flushed, both with running and with anger.

"I hope you're happy!" she exclaimed. "A *D*. A stupid *D*! We're lucky we passed at all—I think Miss Phillips just took pity on us! Or on me, anyway. It's all your fault." She paused, finally at a loss for words.

"A stupid *D*," she repeated.

"Hey, twins!" yelled Karen as she passed them both and waved.

"Oh, shut up!" shouted Rebecca, her cheeks burning. She hated it when her classmates said that. As if she could ever be related to someone like Lonney! But although Lonney was much taller than she was, their brown hair and brown eyes, and even the shape of their faces with high cheekbones, were so similar that their classmates constantly teased them.

"Oh, poor Rebecca got a *D*. Sob, sob," answered Lonney. "My heart is broken."

"That's not all that's gonna be broken," said Rebecca.

"Oh! Oh! Help! Save me! I've been threatened," Lonney cried out in a high voice. "Oh! Somebody help me!" And he began to run around and around Rebecca in a frenzied dance. Rebecca stuck out her leg. Lonney tripped over it and landed in the dirt, flat on his face. He looked up at her, furious. Then suddenly, he started to laugh.

"You should see yourself," he said as he scrambled to his feet. "You look like you're about to die."

"You're just impossible, Lonney. Oh, oh…I give up!" Exasperated, Rebecca turned and began to walk away.

"Yeah," said a resigned voice behind her, "I've heard that lots."

She spun around and faced Lonney. She hated that tone of self-pity, as if none of this was his fault.

"Well, what do you expect?" she replied. "You did everything you could to wreck this project. It could have been great. You missed almost every one of our meetings. You didn't even try!"

"Why should I try?" asked Lonney sullenly. "What difference would it make? Nobody would care. 'How to Improve the School System.' Who would listen anyway? That issue was just a waste of time."

"Well, Miss Phillips would've!" Rebecca exclaimed. "And

9

we could've learned something. And what about your parents? You'll have to show them this D."

A strange expression passed over Lonney's face. "Tell me something," he said, as if trying to change the subject, "if you were so worried about your mark, why didn't you do the stupid thing yourself?"

"Why—why—" she spluttered, "the whole point of our getting stuck together was that we were supposed to learn how to co-operate. Everyone else managed to work together. You don't understand *anything*, do you?"

Lonney paused for a minute and stared at Rebecca. The look was so piercing that Rebecca began to grow uncomfortable.

Honestly, she thought, you'd think I was from another planet—when it's more like he's, well, from another *universe*.

"Look, Rebecca," Lonney said, "I'm sorry you got a D, okay? Now I gotta go." He stepped around her, then strode across the park and down Fleet toward the tracks.

She shook her head as she watched him go.

Lonney was always in trouble. He spent more time in the principal's office than all the rest of the kids in her class put together. Evan had told her that sometimes Lonney refused to put on shorts or a t-shirt for gym. Evan thought Lonney's dad beat him and Lonney didn't want anyone to see the bruises. The one time Lonney showed up for a meeting on the project, he'd fallen asleep. He said he'd been out all night and that he had to sleep sometime.

Rebecca remembered how she had almost died when Miss Phillips put them together for the project. And everything had turned out just as bad as she'd expected. Although—once or twice—Lonney really did seem nice. They'd joke around. He even had a couple of good ideas, but he would throw them out before even trying them, saying, what's the difference? Who cares?

And then he apologizes, just like that! She couldn't figure him out.

She shook her head again, then looked around to see if there was anyone to walk with. The park and the schoolyard were empty now, so she strolled home alone. It was a short walk, down Fleet half a block, then a few houses up on Cordova.

Rebecca explained the D to her mom and dad over supper. They were mildly sympathetic, but her mom wondered why she hadn't just gone ahead and done the project by herself. This made Rebecca furious all over again. First Lonney, then her mother. It was too much. The whole point was that they were supposed to do it *together*. But a little voice inside her said, yeah, but really, why didn't I? To prove to Lonney he couldn't just expect a free ride? And why try to prove anything to him anyway?

For a while after dinner, Rebecca had to concentrate on packing a special lunch for school the next day, so she didn't have time to think about the project. Their class was going on a picnic to Bird's Hill Park. They were celebrating the last day of school, the last year at Brock. Next year they'd all be in junior high.

Her mom came into the kitchen just as she was finishing up and gave Rebecca a kiss.

"Okay, up to bed now, sweetheart. Sleep well."

"Night, Mom."

But when Rebecca tried to sleep, thoughts of Lonney and the stupid project kept her awake. She felt a little bad about that scene in the school yard. Maybe she shouldn't have tripped him. She did have a bad temper, but she never actually got into real physical fights. But this time Lonney deserved it. He'd asked for it. Of course, that's probably what Lonney's dad said when he hit Lonney.

Honestly, Lonney wasn't worth thinking about at all! She wouldn't think about him again. She turned on her light, and read until her eyes hurt, and then fell asleep with the comforting thought that since tomorrow was the last day of school, she at least wouldn't have to see him again until the fall. And maybe, if she were really, really lucky, they'd even be in different classes! Now *that* would be something to hope for!

CHAPTER TWO

O h, I hate this! thought Rebecca, as she turned over in bed. Every morning, every summer, despite blinds and drapes, the sun woke her up. She looked at her watch. Six a.m. She sighed, realizing she'd never get back to sleep.

Slowly, she struggled to get up. Rebecca was not at her best in the morning, to say the least. Groggy and grumpy, she did what she usually did in the summer—she perched herself on the bookshelf which was built in along the back wall of her room, opened the drapes, then flipped up the blind. The sun had just risen and a cool breeze blew through the open screen window. The sky was awash in shades of blue. It was going to be a perfect day.

Her window on the second floor looked over her backyard and rows of streets. Kitty-corner to the house, across the street, was the children's park and the back part of the school yard. Rebecca loved looking down onto the tree-lined streets, a riot of flowers everywhere.

Today, however, something definitely marred the view. A long, dirty, black van was parked on the street below, just opposite the park.

Rebecca realized that this wasn't the first time she'd seen it. It had been there for a few nights now. She wondered who it belonged to. Maybe someone was moving?

Just then, something caught her eye. Someone was walking in the park. As the person came closer, Rebecca could see it was a boy, and the boy began to look very familiar. Yes, she was sure now—it was Lonney. She'd know that flashy black jacket of his anywhere because he'd plastered gold stars all over it.

What was he doing out at this hour? Honestly! She couldn't seem to get rid of him—he was the last person she'd thought about the night before, and now here he was again! She watched him plunk himself down on a swing. He looked sad. Really sad. She couldn't exactly see his expression, but his head was hanging and he kicked at the dirt.

Suddenly she felt awful about her behaviour yesterday. How could she have tripped him like that? His bad behaviour was no excuse for her bad behaviour. She needed to apologize. She slipped out of bed and before she knew it, she was getting dressed. She threw on the jeans and the t-shirt that she'd dropped on her desk chair the night before, and then she crept down the stairs. She grabbed her jacket and jogged down Cordova until she rounded the corner to Fleet Street, That's when she saw Lonney. He was walking past the van. Rebecca lifted her arm to wave at him and was just about to call out when the doors of the black van burst open and two burly, bearded men jumped out. They ran over to Lonney, stuck something in his mouth, picked him up, threw him in the van, slammed the doors shut, and drove down Fleet away from where Rebecca stood.

For a moment Rebecca couldn't quite compute what had happened. Had she just seen Lonney being kidnapped? There was really no other explanation for what had happened. She had to do something!

She sprinted back down Cordova. She was about to burst into her house and yell for her parents to call the police, when suddenly she realized that she had no license plate number or anything that could help the police find the van quickly. It was then that she noticed her bike, lying on the lawn, unlocked, as usual. How many times had her mom nagged her about putting it in the garage or at least locking it up? But it was an old-fashioned bike with only old one speed and apparently not good enough for bicycle thieves. And now she was happy for that. She grabbed the bike and, within seconds, was back on Fleet Street. She would get that license plate number.

And there was the van. It was driving at a sedate pace, perhaps so as not to draw attention, but it was still a good ten blocks away. Then it turned.

Rebecca wasn't sure which block it had turned down but she pedaled as fast as she could until she reached Waverly around ten blocks away from where she'd started. She peered down the street. There was no sign of the van, but of course it could have turned right or left on Grant—or maybe it had turned on another street. What to do? She decided to take a chance and take Waverly. It was a main street and the one they would most likely use. She quickly looked down each street and suddenly caught a glimpse of the van on Taylor St. She turned down Taylor and pedaled as fast as she could. And there it was, parked in the shadows in front of an industrial building, a low one-story affair set well back off the road.

Rebecca brought her bike to a dead stop, jumped off, then pulled it up on the boulevard. There was no movement in the van and none in the building that she could tell. Had they already taken Lonney inside? She reached for her phone and then realized with horror that she'd left it at home. Now what?

She took a breath. She should get close, memorize the license plate and then get home or to a phone at a 7-11 or something and call the police. She left her bike on the boulevard and crossed the street. She walked along a paved driveway and right up to the van. Her heart was pounding. She memorized the plate and was about to sprint away when she heard a muffled shout. Against her best instincts, she peered cautiously into the window by the door of the building.

The two men who had grabbed Lonney were dragging him along so that his legs barely touched the floor. They carried him over to a see-through booth that was in the middle of a large, mostly bare room. They shoved him inside and slammed the door. Rebecca could see Lonney inside the booth, pounding his fists against the walls. Then a third man came out of an office. He gave the kidnappers what looked like a lot of money. He counted out bill after bill. The two men recounted it and then turned to leave. Rebecca slipped around the corner of the building so that she couldn't be seen from the van. She certainly didn't want to join Lonney.

There was a window around the side as well and Rebecca peered in. The man who had paid the kidnappers was very strange looking. His face and neck were a mass of scars and the skin on his cheeks seemed to be almost stitched on in patchwork pieces. The top of his head was also covered in scars, which ran in jagged lines over his completely bald head. He was of medium height, but so emaciated and stooped that he seemed much smaller.

He walked over to the booth where Lonney was still banging against the clear walls. In his hand was some kind of small device, maybe a phone or computer. After working on it for a few moments he looked up from it and waited.

Then Lonney vanished. He was just...gone.

The man turned and walked back into his office.

Rebecca felt suddenly woozy and light-headed. Shaking, she leaned her back against the building, then slid down to the ground.

Maybe it was an optical illusion, she thought, desperately searching for an explanation. Maybe there's a trap door under the booth or behind it and Lonney fell in.

Forcing herself to get up, Rebecca peeked into the window just in time to see the strange man walk into the booth himself and disappear.

Disappear? What on earth was going on?

Rebecca didn't know what to do. If she went to get the police it would take forever for them to get here—if they believed her—and why should they? Lonney was gone! Gone! There was no evidence of anything!

But maybe there was evidence and she just had to find it. Maybe she could find out where they'd gone.

Rebecca went around to the back of the building. She found a door and although it was locked, there was a large dog door in it, probably used in the past for a big guard dog. She crawled through the small opening. Her hair caught on the rusty hinges and she scraped her back, but she managed to squeeze through. She found herself inside the huge, silent warehouse and saw the booth dead ahead.

She reached the entrance of the booth and peered inside. She couldn't see any trap door, but perhaps it worked by pressing a certain spot. She stuck one toe into the booth and pressed on the rough wood floor. Nothing. She thrust the rest of her foot in and pressed. Again, nothing. She put her right leg in. Gingerly, she stepped in with the left. She was fine. She reached out with her right foot and touched the centre.

And everything went black.

CHAPTER THREE

Rebecca was still standing in the booth. But the warehouse had disappeared and she was now in the corner of a white room. The walls were covered in large computer screens flashing images she didn't recognize. She felt queasy and light-headed. Where were the walls of the warehouse?

She stepped out of the booth and sank to her knees, her legs too weak to carry her further. Where was she? She hadn't felt a trapdoor open; she was sure she hadn't fallen. She stared at the strange white room. She could feel the fear inching up her spine like a caterpillar crawling up a tree.

Suddenly she heard voices approaching the closed door of the room.

"How could you leave the machine on like that?" demanded a deep male voice. "Why, anyone could be transported here if they wandered into the machine."

Transported? thought Rebecca.

"I wasn't thinking!" said a strained, tearful male voice. "I was so weak. I needed medicine…attention…"

Rebecca looked around desperately. Where could she hide? The centre of the room was bare. Her only hope was to flatten herself against the wall beside the door.

She pushed herself up and sprinted across the room. The

door banged into her just as she pressed herself against the wall. She could hear one person walking across the room toward the booth, and the other shuffling his feet just inside the room. She held her breath as she stood on tiptoes behind the open door.

"We'll have to send someone else back immediately," said the man with the deep voice, from where he stood by the computers. "You go to the medical centre, I'll find Carla and send her. If someone stumbled in there without our knowing, the whole project could be jeopardized. And you know what that means…"

The door slammed behind them.

They'll be back, Rebecca thought frantically. I've got to get out of here.

She waited until their footsteps had receded and then she opened the door and peeked out.

What Rebecca saw made her want to rub her eyes in disbelief. She was staring at a wide, cobblestoned street. Directly across from her was a quaint old shop with a window display of rings, bracelets, and necklaces. A sign, attached to the shop, hung over the street. On it, written in old-fashioned lettering, was the word *Jewellers*.

She looked up and down the street. The buildings were attached to each other, all only one storey high, and each had a sign hanging out into the street. There were no sidewalks to speak of, the cobblestone coming right up to the front doors. Small potted trees lined the street and a few feet to her right was a little grassy area surrounded by potted trees and bushes. She could hear a bird sing and by the light she judged it to be early morning.

She had no time to examine anything more closely, however. She had to find somewhere to hide. She ran down the street to her left, thankful for her sneakers. Regular shoes would have made too much noise. As she ran, and looked for a hiding place, something nagged at the back of her mind. This place reminded her of something—but what? She ran past a restaurant and a doctor's office on one side, a photographer's and a store with a sign saying *Chemist's* on the other. Abruptly the street turned to the left. It was a short street made up of many small houses all attached to one another. She stopped for a moment, confused. There seemed to be nowhere to hide.

Suddenly, she realized that a door across the street was opening. And before she could react, she was face-to-face with Lonney!

"Lonney!" she gasped. She grasped his hands as if she would never let go. "Oh, I never thought I'd be so happy to see you!"

"Rebecca!" Lonney couldn't believe his eyes, either. "They caught you, too? You're the *last* person I thought they'd get."

"Lonney," Rebecca whispered urgently, "no one caught me. I got here by myself. I saw you being kidnapped. I found the van. I—"

"Are you telling me that no one knows you're here?"

Rebecca nodded.

He shook his head in disbelief. "But how did you get here?"

She had just opened her mouth to answer when he stopped her.

"No, tell me later. We've got to hide you. Once they know you're here, you'll be as trapped as we are. But if we can keep you free—maybe you can help get us out of here. Wherever here is," he muttered. "C'mon." He grabbed her by the wrist and dragged her down to where the street abruptly ended in front of a giant door. It was painted blue, so that until they were up close to it, Rebecca thought it was blue sky. Lonney pushed a red button by the side of the door and it slid slowly open. Rebecca gasped.

She was facing a huge, round cavern hewn out of rock. The entire floor was taken up by three large, square pools, each one the size of a hockey rink. The pools were filled with water. Narrow walkways, also made of rock, traversed the cavern.

"C'mon!" urged Lonney. But Rebecca was rooted to the spot, thunderstruck. When she'd first seen the white room, she had been sure she was inside a building. Then she discovered that she was outside, but in a town that looked like it was a hundred years old or something. Now she was staring at the opening of an underground cave! She was so disoriented she could hardly breathe. Was she inside or outside? Or was she underground? How could she be both places at once?

Lonney looked at her sympathetically and, putting his arm around her back, gently pushed her into the cave. He pressed a red button on the inside rock wall and the heavy blue door slid shut.

"No one ever comes here," Lonney said. "This is their water source, but it's all piped and it never seems to break down. The first night I was here I checked the whole place out and found this. Sometimes I come here when everyone is sleeping just to breathe in the smell of the water."

"What do you mean the first night?" Rebecca managed to get out. "They took you only minutes ago."

"I've been here for a week," Lonney answered.

That made no sense to Rebecca. She frowned.

"Look, if I'm missing they'll come looking for me," Lonney answered, "and they might find you. I've got to get back. It's almost breakfast time. Or what they call breakfast. I'll have to wait 'til tonight when everyone's asleep. Then I'll sneak back here. And I'll tell you everything I know."

"Tonight!" Rebecca exclaimed in horror. "You're not going to leave me here all alone until tonight! I'll go crazy. I don't even know what I'm doing here, where we are..."

"Neither do I," Lonney replied. "One thing I can tell you, though. All those old-fashioned buildings out there...they're fake. It took me a while to figure it out 'cause they've done it so well—but it's all fake. The buildings aren't buildings at all—it's like a Hollywood set. You go inside any one of them and you'll find one room. If it's the restaurant you'll find a dining room, the doctor's office is an examining room, the jeweller's is a tool shop—and there's never more than one room."

"'That's it," said Rebecca, "I knew it reminded me of something. The Museum of Man and Nature. They have a whole city built just like it was in Winnipeg in the 1920s. I've been there so often." She shook her head and started to bite her nails, a habit she thought she had finally broken only months before.

"But why?" she said, looking at Lonney. "Who would go to all the trouble?" She paused. "And where? I mean, we must be underground—"

"We'll try to figure it out later," said Lonney. "Together." He gave her a fleeting smile of encouragement. "Don't worry, I'll be back."

She smiled weakly. "You know," she sighed, "I think that's the first time I've ever seen you really smile. Takes a lot to get one out of you, doesn't it?"

Then he grinned. "Nothing like being kidnapped to bring out the best in you."

She looked at him in amazement. He'd been nicer to her in the last five minutes than he'd been all year at school. He turned and pressed the button beside the door. It slid open and Lonney stepped through, pushing the button on the other side of the door to close it.

Rebecca sat down on the cold stone floor beside the door. She stared at the pool of water in front of her. It was a greyish colour, reflecting the grey stone above and around it. She couldn't see the source of the light but it was bright in the cave—bright grey—a pretty unusual combination. The water was smooth except for bubbles at the far end of the pools, and it was almost level with the stone floor. Rebecca reached over and stuck her hand in. It was cold. She put a finger in her mouth and tasted the water. It tasted just like water. Somehow she thought maybe it would all turn out to be imaginary, unreal. She leaned back against the hard rock wall. It was all so—bizarre. Obviously they were underground. But where? And more important, why? Well, she'd just have to wait for Lonney to get back before she could find out. She sighed and stared at the giant pools of water. At least she wouldn't be thirsty.

CHAPTER FOUR

"Wake up. Wake up. Rebecca, Rebecca, Rebecca." The sound floated toward Rebecca from far away. She really didn't want to wake up. Something told her it was much cosier, much safer, to remain asleep. She was having such a nice dream. She was eating supper at home. There was carrot cake with vanilla icing for dessert. Everyone was laughing and talking.

"Go away," she mumbled.

"Rebecca," hissed a voice in her ear. "Get up."

Rebecca's eyes flew open. She was wide awake. And scared.

"Oh, Lonney," she sighed with relief, "it's you. I must've dozed off." She looked at her watch. It was 11:45 p.m.

"Here," he said, kneeling beside her, "I've brought you some food." He handed her two shiny black pills.

"You've got to be kidding!" she exclaimed. "I'm starved. I haven't eaten all day and you bring me pills! I don't have a headache, I'm hungry."

"I said I'd bring you something to eat, didn't I? It's their food." He pulled a small, transparent cup from his pocket, dipped it in the water and handed it to her.

She hesitated.

"It's these pills or starvation."

Rebecca looked suspiciously at the pills in the palm of her hand. Then she shrugged, popped them in her mouth, took a gulp of water, and downed them. "Wonderful," she said.

"We do get one meal a day of what they call real food," Lonney grimaced. "Dried stuff you mix with water. Instant protein, instant carbohydrates, they say. It's almost worse than the pills."

"Okay" said Rebecca, "let's forget the food. I want you to tell me everything you know."

"It's like a bad dream," Lonney replied, shaking his head. "Really, I can't believe any of this has happened. Truth is, I haven't the faintest where we are or why. All I know is one minute I'm walking through the park, the next minute some guys grab me, take me to this warehouse, throw me in some kind of booth, and then suddenly, somehow, I'm somewhere else! And there's this old guy trying hard to be nice, telling me everything's going to be fine, you know. Well, I've heard that often enough— when adults say everything's great, just don't worry, and don't ask questions—that's how you know it's time to worry. He introduced me to some other adults and the others who have been kidnapped—so far, four other boys, four other girls. One of the adults—Laura—she takes us to a place called The Inn. Outside it's old-fashioned, but you should see the inside! Like something out of a sci-fi movie. She gives us each a glass of water and those pills. I didn't take them that first day. No way. But then I got so hungry—and it didn't seem to hurt the others who took them, so finally I gave in the next day."

"Look," interrupted Rebecca. "That's another thing I don't understand. What do you mean 'the first day?' How long have you been here? I know that I saw you disappear *this morning!*"

"You got me there," answered Lonney, shaking his head. "I've been here for a week. Other kids have been here for even longer. Turns out the other kids who have been kidnapped are kids that won't be missed too soon, kids that were just hanging around the parks or the streets. These people sure don't want anyone in Winnipeg to realize what's happening. Oh, but there are also four kids here who seem to be from here—Lewis, Catherine, Ken, and Iris. Lewis and Catherine are about our age. Ken and Iris are younger—maybe ten. They get lessons and they're always in the computer room.

"Laura says we're going to be starting classes soon, too. Classes! 'On what?' I ask her. 'You'll find out soon,' she says. 'Will you ever let us go?' I ask. No answer. They won't, you know. I can tell that whatever this is, it's not for ransom or anything like that. They want us here for some reason."

"Lonney, you've been all over this place, right?" said Rebecca. "Have you found any way out?"

He shook his head. "Only that booth, and although I've managed to sneak back in there, I can't for the life if me figure out how it works. Somehow it got us here, right? But how?"

"Is everyone asleep now?" asked Rebecca.

"It's midnight," replied Lonney, "and I never hear anyone walking around this late. I'm often up 'cause I just can't sleep here."

"Let's go then," said Rebecca. "I want to take a look. Maybe we can find out something about where we are. Maybe we can use that machine to get out of here."

She and Lonney got up. Lonney pushed the red button, the

door slid open, and they walked onto the cobblestone street. It appeared to be night. Two street lamps glowed softly, lighting their way. It looked just as Rebecca would imagine any residential street would have looked in the olden days, late at night.

They passed about three small houses when they heard footsteps coming toward them from the main street.

"Oh, no!" whispered Rebecca.

"This way," said Lonney. "Quick!" and he opened the door nearest them. They dived into a darkened room and shut the door. The footsteps came closer and closer. They were afraid to move for fear of bumping into something.

Click. The door opened. The light was switched on. Rebecca recognized the man from the warehouse immediately. Without warning, Lonney lowered his head and charged right into the man's stomach. The man doubled over with a moan and sank to the floor.

"Let's get out of here," said Lonney, grabbing Rebecca's wrist.

"No," she said quickly, "wait. He'll call for help and the whole place will be looking for us." She looked around frantically. They were in what appeared to be a large storeroom filled with boxes, crates, machine parts, and ropes.

"Ropes!" exclaimed Rebecca. "Come on, we'll tie him up." She grabbed a thin white rope and handed one end of it to Lonney. The man was still on the floor, panting heavily, trying to get up. He seemed very weak. Although he tried to resist them, he could not. They tied his wrists together and his ankles, and propped him up with his back against the wall.

"Don't we have to gag him now?" said Rebecca. "I mean, if

we're going to do this we'd better do it right."

"Look around," said Lonney. "But hurry. He's starting to get his wind back."

"No, no," came the weak voice, "no need to gag me. I won't call out. No one wants to hurt you, believe me."

Rebecca was looking up and down the rows of boxes. "There must be something." She looked at Lonney more closely.

"What about your scarf?" she said.

Lonney always wore a starred kerchief around his neck. It matched his jacket. He grimaced and yanked it off.

"No, wait, don't gag me," pleaded the man. "Let me go and you go back to your rooms. I won't tell anyone. This isn't a jail, you know."

"Could have fooled me!" Lonney exclaimed.

Rebecca stared at their captive. "Tell us what's really going on here, if you don't want us to gag you!"

She could barely look at the man now that she saw him up close. His face was so badly scarred that even his lips and nose were deformed. The man's eyes began to water. His lower lip trembled.

"You won't want to hear this. I can hardly bear to tell you… but I know the others were going to tell you soon anyway. Just a minute," he said, looking at Rebecca intently, "are you new? Who brought you in? I don't remember seeing you before."

"Never mind that," ordered Lonney. "Just tell us where we are and why we're here."

"Well," the man said, "you're in an underground, top-secret, scientific complex. The government built this many years ago, in the year 2020, to be exact."

Rebecca and Lonney looked at each other. Lonney rolled

his eyes. "Oh, sure," he said, "we believe you."

"Why would I lie?" said the man, looking at them both. "No, of course you don't believe me," he added, shaking his head. "But I wouldn't lie, not about this."

Something about his tone made Rebecca feel very uncomfortable.

"The year 2020," the man repeated. "Of course the look of this place must confuse you. But they wanted to create an environment that people could live and work in for many years, underground, without becoming depressed. Something nostalgic and restful. Grey, windowless concrete is so depressing, don't you think? In fact, I was one of the consulting psychiatrists. I was on call for this base. Mind you, I lived on the surface—that's why I look the way I do. I was on top when it happened..." His voice trailed off. Tears began to trickle down his cheeks. "It was twenty years ago. Seems like yesterday..."

He took a deep breath and continued. "You see, no one thought it could happen. Not really. It was all over so fast...I was visiting friends up top in Churchill. It was targeted because of the runway. I walked back here after it happened. I don't know how long it took me. Winnipeg was hit, of course...All cities with large enough runways to carry bombers were targeted... This base was far enough north that it was spared the worst."

Rebecca broke out in a cold sweat. She reached for Lonney's hand and held onto it as if it could keep her alive and sane. It must all be a lie. What he was saying *couldn't* be true.

"I saw it all as I walked. People stuck with shards of glass and metal, still alive. Bones sticking out, but still alive. There was a heat blast, of course. Then the firestorms. People with skin burned off, but still alive. Animals, all blind. I'm a doctor. I couldn't help. No one could help. No hospitals, no medicine left. I walked past it all, saw all the people dying. The few left that weren't vaporized, crushed, or burned to death suffered fatal doses of radiation.

"There were others like myself. Not killed outright. Able to walk. But most had nowhere to go. They must have died a slow, horrible death. I had radiation sickness. Nausea, dizziness, vomiting blood all the time, coughing up blood. Somehow I made it back here. I had two small children, Justin and Anna. My wife. My four brothers. Their children. All in Winnipeg. I only hope they died quickly. I finally found my way to the entrance and made it down here. The scientists down here were all right. The air is purified, and so is the water. A few of us made it back here. We knew we could get help down here. Of course I'm dying now. Leukemia.

"The worst part was not knowing. All communication was wiped out. From what I saw, I think it was a global war— but of course, we can't know for sure. If it was, we may never be able to go back to the surface. The ozone layer would be gone. The sun would cook you to a crisp. But before that happened there was probably a nuclear winter. The dust and fallout from the blast would have created a cloud. The cloud would have blocked the sun. The temperature would have dropped all over the world and all the crops would have died. Billions would have starved to death."

"So what's up there now?" asked Lonney, shakily.

"Mostly bones, I guess. And bacteria. The bacteria would have fed on the corpses. And then the bacteria would have mutated. The few people left, those that didn't die from radiation or starvation, anyone not in a shelter like this, probably would have died from plague, cholera, and polio. Diseases that can't be treated anymore because there's no medicine, no doctors. Or they may have contracted brand new diseases. And maybe it wasn't only nuclear—maybe there were chemical weapons, biological weapons used first and that escalated the fight until they used nuclear warheads.

"We've tried to figure out how it started. Was it terrorists? Was it some small country willing to start a war because they wanted their neighbour's resources? Or did it start with a nuclear accident? I don't suppose it matters now. Sometimes I wonder why I made such an effort to survive."

Rebecca felt numb inside. "I don't believe you," she whispered.

"But," said the man, seeming not to hear her, "we'll save you now. If you stay in Winnipeg, you'll be killed, won't you? But not now. No, not now. You see, this top-secret installation was built because the greatest minds in the world were here doing research on time travel. Everyone who was here at the time of the blast is fine. There are air purifiers here, and it was far enough away from the nearest blast that they weren't suffocated like most people in shelters. I made my way here…They let me in. They knew me." His voice trailed off.

"No," breathed Rebecca, "it's not possible. None of it is possible. I will wake up! I will!"

The man looked at her with great sympathy.

"I'm a doctor," he said gently, "a psychiatrist. I know what you're feeling now. But there's no use trying to deny it. It's real— all of it. This is no dream. They've perfected the time machine they were working on and now you've been brought here, into the year 2050."

"But why?" asked Rebecca.

He replied, "Only those who weren't on the surface when the bombs exploded were able to have healthy children. We only have four children here to date. Anyone who was on the surface, like me, produce children who die before they are born or shortly after. If we don't have more children the human race could die out.

"But," he said, his eyes brightening just a bit, "you'll help us start a new world. We'll bring young, healthy children here from before the war, and you can help us expand this underground complex. We'll make a whole underground city. We can start all over."

"Underground," murmured Lonney. "Never able to see the sky again? What kind of life is that?"

"It's the only kind," said the man, heaving a great sigh. "The only kind left." Rebecca and Lonney had been listening so intently that they hadn't heard the approaching footsteps. Suddenly the door was flung open and four adults rushed in. Rebecca and Lonney looked at each other in dismay. Now she was caught, too!

CHAPTER FIVE

"What's going on here?" exclaimed an attractive, petite woman, whom Rebecca judged to be about her mother's age, forty or so. "Daniel, we've been looking all over for you. Why is he tied up?" She turned to Lonney.

"They meant no harm, Laura," said Daniel. "You can't blame them..."

Laura untied him and helped him to his feet. The other three adults who had crowded into the storeroom with Laura were men. Two of them seemed very old; the other was so badly scarred it was impossible to tell whether he was young or old. He was also missing an arm.

Laura stared at Rebecca.

"I know every child we've brought here," she stated, "and I don't know this one."

Rebecca looked at Lonney in despair. Their secret would come out now and they'd never, ever get home.

"Who are you?" demanded Laura.

"That's none of your business!" Rebecca shot back. She could feel herself getting hot and flushed with anger. "How dare you stand there and talk to me as if you had a right to know anything! How dare you! First you blow up the world, then you think you can make everything right by kidnapping innocent children. You're no better than common criminals. What right do you have to decide what's best for us?" Rebecca started to cry. "The whole world destroyed and..."

"It wasn't us who blew up the world," objected Laura. "How could you accuse us of that?"

"Well, you didn't stop it, did you?" Rebecca shouted. "So I say it's your fault."

"You didn't stop it either, did you?" replied Laura softly. "Remember, this is 2050. In 2030, you would have been an adult. Why didn't you stop it?" That idea shocked Rebecca so much that she stopped crying and just stared at Laura, at a loss for words.

"Now," said one of the two older men, "you tell us who you are and what you're doing here."

Rebecca glared at them all. She refused to answer.

"It must have happened when you left the machine on, Dan," said one of the old men.

"Yes, I followed him here," admitted Rebecca. "But I told the police first," she declared. "And they'll be here soon to rescue us all!"

Laura shook her head.

"Carla has taken over for Dan," she said, "and there's no trouble. No one knows anything."

"What's your name?" asked Laura.

Rebecca remained silent.

"You're upset now, of course," said Laura. "Obviously Dan has told you everything. But soon you'll realize that you are one of the lucky ones. And you'll thank us. Come along now. I'll take you to your room. Lonney, go to bed, please. You have a busy day tomorrow. Classes begin."

Lonney looked at Rebecca and shrugged his shoulders.

As he shuffled past her, he whispered under his breath, "The cave, two hours."

"What was that?" asked Laura sharply.

"I said, be brave, little flower," said Lonney with a sweet smile. Rebecca, who only seconds before felt she would never laugh again, laughed in spite of herself. Never in her wildest dreams could she have imagined Lonney saying anything so mushy.

"He always calls me little flower," she said to Laura confidentially as they walked onto the street. For a moment, she enjoyed the game. It gave her some little sense of power to be able to fool this adult, if only for a moment.

They walked toward the main street, then Laura opened the door to one of the houses and motioned for Rebecca to go in ahead of her. It was dark inside. Laura turned on the light. Rebecca counted eight beds in the room; four were occupied. As the light flashed on, four girls sat up in their beds, one letting out a small scream.

"It's just a new friend, girls," said Laura. "Get her settled, then go back to sleep. We have a busy day tomorrow." Then she turned and left.

The girls crowded around Rebecca. They all talked at once, wanting to know where she'd been captured and how. Did she know where they were, what was happening?

Rebecca sat down on a cot and told the girls her story right from the beginning. Then she took a deep breath and told them why they were there. When she had finished, she began asking the group about themselves.

Blair, a large girl with black hair which seemed to shoot off every which way, introduced herself and the others: Lindsay, a small fair girl; Ellen, tall and thin; and Sue, also very tall. Both Ellen and Sue started to cry.

Blair told Rebecca that each of them had been wandering around a city park in the early morning when they were abducted. They'd all been runaways many times before, so although their absence would no doubt be reported to the police, everyone, including their parents, would assume they'd just run away again.

Rebecca could see that their captors were being very careful not to cause any alarm in the city. But what about her own parents? They would certainly be frantic. They would have the police, the RCMP, everyone in the city out looking for her. Maybe there was hope.

No one felt like sleeping, but no one felt like talking either. They sat on their cots with the lights on, and tried to wrap their heads around the fact that the world as they understood it was gone. Destroyed. Rebecca looked at her watch every few minutes, barely able to wait until it was time to meet Lonney. Patience was not her strong point and now she could hardly sit still. One by one, the other girls drifted off to sleep. At last, the two hours elapsed and it was time to leave.

She flicked off the light, then cautiously opened the door. All was quiet. It looked just like night out—she could even see some stars twinkling in the fake sky. The street lamps glowed softly. It certainly was realistic, Rebecca thought. Even the air had the cool tang of night.

She pulled the door shut behind her and ran down the street toward the cave. She pressed the red button. The door opened. Lonney was standing on the other side. She stepped into the cave and he pressed the button in the cave to close the door.

For a moment, their eyes met. The story they had just heard, the explanation of why they were there, was worse, much worse, than anything either of them had imagined. Lonney's eyes were red and swollen. Rebecca could see he had been crying. She tried to wipe away some fresh tears of her own.

"I don't think we'd better stay long," was the first thing Lonney said. "They've already checked my room once. They'll be keeping a close eye on us."

Rebecca nodded. "Well, at least they don't lock us up," she said.

"No," he answered, "they don't have to. There's nowhere for us to go."

"That's not true. There *is* somewhere for us to go. Home. And somehow we're going to get there."

"How?"

"I don't know. But if they can go back and forth so can we. We'll have to watch them and see how they use that time machine. And then use it ourselves. Or maybe one of them will agree with us or feel sorry for us and help us."

At this, Lonney snorted and shook his head.

"Well," Rebecca insisted, "we have to be willing to try everything. What about those kids? The four you mentioned, I mean. They might help us—you never know."

"Let's try to meet here every night at two a.m.," said Lonney. Rebecca looked at her watch.

"Is their time the same as ours?"

"It seems to be," Lonney replied. "They keep day and night and try to make it all seem normal somehow. And when I arrived, their time was the same as the time on my watch. Although I still can't figure out how I got here a week ahead of you."

"It must have something to do with the way their time machine works," said Rebecca. "Though it's still hard to believe this whole time-travel story."

"No kidding," said Lonney. "Still, in some weird way, I believe them. I have a pretty good sense of when someone is lying."

Rebecca figured he probably did. "Can you set the alarm on your watch for two a.m. meetings?" she asked.

Lonney nodded.

"I will, too," she said.

"Let's go, then," Lonney said. "See you in the morning."

"Right," said Rebecca.

"Oh, and uh…" Lonney hesitated. "Thanks."

"What for?" asked Rebecca.

"For coming after me," muttered Lonney, looking at his feet. "That was all right."

Rebecca paused. She remembered lying in bed, fuming over Lonney. She remembered hating him. She could feel herself blushing. In fact, she was blushing so much she thought she must be almost turning purple. She pushed the button, opening the door.

"See you," she called over her shoulder as she ran out the

door and down the street, back to the room she'd been assigned to. She opened the door, but it was so dark she couldn't move once she was inside.

"Turn on the light," came a voice. Rebecca fumbled around until she found it.

"Good, it's you," said Blair with relief. "Tell us what's going on."

"Not much yet," said Rebecca. "But Lonney and I are going to meet every night at two. And we are going to figure out a way to get out of here."

The way the girls looked at her, then away from her, made it clear to Rebecca that they didn't have much hope. Rebecca lay down on an empty cot. She was sure she would never sleep, but within minutes she fell into a light, fitful sleep, filled with strange and terrifying dreams.

CHAPTER SIX

"Everybody up!" Laura stood in the doorway. "The dining room in ten minutes, please!"

The five girls dragged themselves out of bed, and took turns washing in the small bathroom adjacent to their room. There was only one sink. Blair explained to Rebecca that the showers were in a larger bathroom down the hall. The only clothes they had were the jeans and tops they'd all been wearing when they had been captured.

They each took turns using the comb Blair always kept in her jeans pocket. Rebecca's hair was easy to take care of—she wore it in a short, blunt cut because she hated having to fuss. The girls were too tired after being up half the night to make the effort to talk to each other, so they prepared for the day in silence.

They met the boys in the street. Lonney introduced Rebecca to the four boys—Robert, Mike, Paul, and Nathan—then they all walked together to the dining room.

It had a large, old-fashioned sign saying *The Inn* over the door, but the inside was anything but old-fashioned.

Everything was bright and shiny. The tables were low and rectangular, made of different shades of tinted plastic, perched on slim legs tinted the same colour. Deep reds, blues, and yellows were the dominant colours. The chairs were also made of the same material. They had slim, L-shaped contours which fit under the tables.

It was a large room with perhaps twenty tables, each large enough for eight people. Four tables at the front of the room had been set up, one behind the other, so that all the chairs faced front. Food pills were neatly laid out beside tall glasses of water on all the tables.

The kids sat down at the last three tables and swallowed their pills. Soon, four more kids, all dressed in grey pants and tops, entered. Rebecca watched them with interest. Lonney, who was sitting beside her, whispered to her.

"That's Lewis—he always comes in first—then Catherine, then Kent and Iris."

Lewis was a tall boy with a square-jawed, pale face and deep blue eyes. He had black, wavy hair down to his shoulders, which he wore parted in the middle. He had a straight nose and wide lips. He walked with jerky motions and his eyes flashed around the room, trying to take in everything.

Catherine was also tall, with flowing red hair, bright blue eyes, a turned-up nose, and a full mouth. She seemed to glide into the room, her head tilted up, her feet barely touching the floor.

Kent and Iris, by comparison, were far less striking. Kent was average height with short brown hair, light brown eyes, and a round, pleasant face. Iris was short and thin. She was very pale, with short blond hair, pretty green eyes, and a small, heart-shaped face. They took their places at the front tables.

When all was quiet again in the dining room, an old man

entered. He stood, hands in pockets, looking at the children.

"My name," he began, "is Phillip. I know that you must have heard what has happened and why you are here. I know how hard it must be for all of you—perhaps you would rather not believe what you've been told. It was even harder for us to comprehend—not only the loss of all those we loved, but the loss of the human race. But now, with the development of time travel, we dare to hope again. And you children are that hope.

"Today, we will begin your education. And soon you will be able to help us build a better future. We need more space. A better living environment. We have some tools and machinery. Others we will have to build from scratch. You will all be trained in the use of these tools and machines. Together, we will build a beautiful underground city. As we bring more children from the past, we will eventually have a vast underground nation. This is a great project and a great opportunity here before us. It is time to look forward."

Rebecca leapt to her feet.

"I don't know about the others," she exclaimed, "but I don't want to help with your project, I want to go home! And if you don't send me back, it won't do you any good keeping me here. You can't force me to learn, and you can't force me to work your stupid machines."

And she sat down.

Lonney looked at her with surprise. "What a great idea," he said with admiration. "You're right. They can't force us to learn or to work. Boy, if anyone knows that, it's me." He laughed. He leaned back on his chair, put his feet up, and crossed his arms. He began to hum a tune under his breath.

For a moment, the other kids looked bewildered. But one by one they followed Rebecca and Lonney until no one was paying any attention. Their feet were up on the tables and they were all humming.

But up at the front of the room, Lewis jumped to his feet.

"What's the matter with you all?" he raged. "You don't know how lucky you are! It would serve you right if we sent you back and took others. Then you could die in misery, just as you deserve."

A few of the kids looked around at the others, hesitated, and then sat up straight again. He had a point. Just then Laura and Dan entered the room and stood near the door, watching with interest.

Rebecca could see that Lewis was someone to be reckoned with. She stood up, forcing herself to seem casual and in control. Actually her heart was pounding so hard she could barely breathe. She knew that this was a crucial moment.

"Well," she said, faking a yawn and a stretch, "there's no use hanging around here. I'm going into that other room. I can see they have video games and everything in there."

Lonney jumped up from his chair. "Great idea, let's go!" he said.

The others moved from their chairs and followed Rebecca and Lonney out of the dining room, leaving Lewis standing at his table.

Rebecca could hear Dan talking to Laura as they left. She strained to hear and caught the first part of what he was saying— "Don't worry, give them time. They'll come 'round..."

Rebecca led the way into a large recreation room. There were six computers, a ping-pong table, a pool table, a small shelf of books with chairs close to it, an audio player with discs and some iPods and iPads.

"Some things never change," Rebecca commented.

"Oh yeah?" answered Lonney. "Wait till you see these games. They're three-dimensional holograms." He was already at the computers, looking at the different displays. Rebecca watched him and the others play for awhile but then got bored. She noticed that Catherine, Kent, and Iris were sitting at a table in the dining room, studying. Rebecca approached them.

"Hi," she said, tentatively.

They looked up. Kent and Iris viewed her with interest and said, "Hi." Catherine's expression remained decidedly cool.

Rebecca sat down with them.

"What was it like before?" Iris blurted out, as if she'd been dying to ask that question for the longest time.

Rebecca was taken aback.

"What was *what* like?" she said.

"The world," said Catherine, trying not to seem too eager, but obviously burning with curiosity. "What was it like to live on the surface?"

Rebecca looked at them, trying to hide the pity she suddenly felt.

"You just can't imagine," she said, "how beautiful the earth is. Or was—or..." She stopped. She could feel the tears coming again. "The sun, the air, the lakes, the rivers, the flowers..." She couldn't go on because she knew she would start to cry if she did.

45

She felt she was in mourning for the entire world.

"Look," she said to the three kids, "you've got to help us get back. You've got to. Do any of you know how the time machine works?"

Iris and Kent shot a quick glance at Catherine, then looked down at the table. It was a small gesture, but Rebecca didn't miss it.

"Catherine, you know, don't you? You can help us. You must see that this is not a solution. This isn't right. People weren't made to live this way, underground…"

"How can you say that?" Catherine responded, leaning forward and looking into Rebecca's eyes. "I can't help you—it would be wrong. This is the only hope left for the survival of the human race. Maybe, after hundreds of years, the earth will renew itself—at least enough for us to go back up to the surface. But there won't be any people left if you don't stay here now. Don't you see?"

Rebecca slumped into her chair. Maybe she was being selfish. Maybe she'd have to be strong, to say goodbye to the earth and everyone and everything she loved on it, so she could stay here and help build another world. Of course, she'd be missed, but what was one person—or twenty, or even fifty?

But wait! She sat up straight in her chair. A thought suddenly flashed through her and electrified her whole being.

She put her hand on Catherine's arm and leaned forward.

"Show us how to go back," she said, looking right at Catherine, "Then Lonney and I and the other kids can work to stop the war from ever happening!"

Catherine shook off Rebecca's hand with a derisive laugh.

"What do you mean?" she said. "That's the silliest thing I've ever heard."

"Is it?" said Rebecca, almost to herself. "Is it?" She got up and began to pace up and down.

"Have you studied history?"

"Of course," Catherine replied.

"Not too long ago," Rebecca said, "we were studying the Nazi era in school. Ever heard of it?"

"Yes."

"And we learned about this Swedish man, Raoul Wallenburg. He saved a hundred thousand Jews all by himself. One man. I kept thinking, if there'd only been another hundred like him, or even...Don't you see?" she exclaimed, turning to face the kids. She leaned over the table. "You don't know the difference one person can make. You take me, Lonney, the others away...You don't know what effect that can have. Laura asked me before why I hadn't stopped it. But maybe I didn't realize. Now, knowing what the future will be, if I go back, I could work to stop it from ever happening. Maybe if we all went back now, we could do that. We have to go back and *do* something. Don't you see?"

"But," said Catherine, rising to face her, "what if you go back and you can't change anything?"

Rebecca couldn't think of an answer. It was a horrifying thought. She noticed that Lonney had joined them and was listening intently. Then he chimed in.

"What if taking us away helped *make* the disaster?"

Rebecca stared at him. Could a few kids make that much difference? Why not?

"You know, Cath," boomed Lewis's voice from behind Rebecca, "they might have a point."

Lewis walked over to the table. "You're not quite as stupid as I thought at first," he said to Rebecca.

"Wish I could say the same thing to you," she retorted.

He glared at her. "What you said could make sense. It's possible..."

"Then you have to help us," Rebecca urged. "We have to know how to work that time machine so we can get out of here."

"I don't know," said Lewis, "I have to think about it." He paused. "The adults would never go for it." He paused again. "We'll think about it," he said, looking at Catherine.

Rebecca could tell by his tone of voice that he was stubborn and there was no point in pushing him.

"Okay," she said, "but don't think too long. Tonight after supper. All right?"

"We could meet in the recreation room at eight," Lewis suggested. "The adults always have a meeting in an office down the street at that time."

Just then Laura walked in.

"Well, well," she said, smiling broadly. "It's nice to see you're all getting to know one another. It's time for the morning workout, though, so let's go."

The kids fell into groups with their friends and followed Laura down the main street. They stopped in front of a door with a large picture of a body builder in a 1920s swimsuit painted on it.

Over the door hung a huge sign which said "Gym." As she walked through the door, Rebecca was amazed to find a large room containing a big, square swimming pool surrounded by potted palms. There were flowers everywhere. It was quite charming. The girls went into a common dressing room to change. Laura gave each girl a swimsuit. The swimsuit consisted of a pair of grey boxer shorts attached to a grey camisole. Rebecca had seen pictures of 1920 bathing suits that looked something like these.

She felt herself blush at the thought of Lonney seeing her in this ridiculous outfit. But when she got out to the pool, she discovered that the boys looked even sillier because they were wearing the exact same thing. She started to giggle and then Lonney, who looked very embarrassed, laughed and jumped straight into the pool. He called to Rebecca, "Come on, it's great!"

She stuck in a toe. Cold. Very cold. She took a deep breath and jumped in close to Lonney, creating a huge splash which hit him right in the face. He splashed her in revenge. Blair came to her rescue, and soon they were all involved in a big water fight. All except Lewis, Catherine, Iris, and Kent, who were in a far corner of the pool, diligently swimming short laps. They probably don't even know how to play, thought Rebecca with pity, as she noticed their serious behaviour. But just then Lonney splashed her full in the face and she had something serious of her own to attend to—namely, paying him back.

CHAPTER SEVEN

The rest of the day dragged by, every moment seeming like hours to Rebecca. After the kids swam, they were given lunch. More pills and water. Rebecca hadn't realized how many pleasurable hours she had spent eating meals and snacks. She missed the tastes and the conversation which usually surrounded the eating of real food. She had to admit, however, she never felt hungry.

After lunch there was a play period, then another attempt to get the kids to study. When this failed, they were once again taken to the pool and, finally, back to the dining room. Something that was almost like food was then served for supper—mushy white stuff, mushy green stuff, and mushy brown stuff—all powdered food mixed with water. It was, apparently, part of a fifty-year supply that had been stored in the complex, just in case. Rebecca thought it was simply the worst mess she'd ever eaten and began wishing they could have the pills instead.

Throughout the day, Rebecca kept thinking of what it meant to change the future. What if they did succeed in avoiding World War III—would this future no longer exist? What would happen to the people here? She shook her head. It was too hard to think through all the possibilities. No, the only way was to get back to her own present. If only Catherine and Lewis would help them! It was their only hope.

Finally the adults departed for their nightly meeting and the kids were left alone in the dining room.

Catherine and Lewis joined Rebecca and Lonney at a table.

"Well?" said Rebecca, "what have you decided?"

Lewis leaned forward. "We'll help you," he said.

Rebecca let out a small sigh of relief. She looked at Lonney. She could see that he too was pleased.

"On one condition," Lewis continued.

"What's that?" she asked warily.

"You take Cath and me with you," he replied.

"What!" Rebecca and Lonney exclaimed together.

"You heard him," said Catherine. "The two of us go or no one goes."

"But why?" said Rebecca. "What about your families?" She paused. "What if we can't do anything and you're killed?"

"We've thought about that," answered Lewis. "We know the day it's supposed to happen. If things haven't changed by then, well, we'll come back here."

Rebecca shook her head. "That means you would meet your parents but you wouldn't have even been born yet," she said. "And you'll be older than they are." She paused. "Who are your parents, anyway?"

"Laura and Stewart," responded Catherine.

"Phillip and Carla," said Lewis.

"But why do you want to come?" Rebecca persisted.

"Because," declared Lewis, "there's nothing for me to do here. I need a challenge. Something big. Something...I heard you talking to Cath about politics. Now I think that might be for me. I could become a great leader of men, I know it!"

Rebecca looked at him thoughtfully, "If you chose to lead our governments away from all the chemical and biological weapons and tried to get the nuclear weapons destroyed, maybe you could do a lot—a whole lot."

"That's what I'd do!" exclaimed Lewis. "I could help prevent all this. And Cath here is a real science wiz—and she could share all the things we've learned here—"

"That's right," Catherine interrupted. "We know how to do without nuclear energy and how to dispose of the nuclear waste you already have. I could use that information to help persuade people to dismantle the nuclear industry."

"If anyone would listen to you," Lonney muttered.

Rebecca chose to ignore the comment.

"I've got to give you two credit," she said to Lewis and Catherine. "You have really thought it out. But where would you live?"

"Uh-oh," interrupted Lonney, "looks like the meeting is finished. Here comes Laura."

"Okay," said Rebecca, "Lonney and I have a secret meeting place—the underground water caves. We'll meet you there at two a.m. and we'll make a plan."

Then everyone went to their sleeping quarters and to bed.

Rebecca immediately fell into a deep sleep, no doubt brought about by both mental and physical exhaustion. Her alarm didn't fail her, however, and after a few hours, she woke with a start and sat up in bed. She had left her jeans on so she wouldn't have to change. After putting on her shoes, she snuck out to the hall.

Looking nervously around, listening for the slightest sound, she sprinted to the end of the street and pushed the red button. The door slid open and she slipped inside.

"Hi!" said Lonney.

"Hi!" said Rebecca. "How long've you been here?"

"Oh, quite a while," he said. "Couldn't sleep."

She nodded sympathetically.

"I can see why you come here," she said in a hushed voice. "It's so quiet, so peaceful. You can almost forget about… everything."

He nodded and they began to wander around the pools, not talking, just waiting for Catherine and Lewis. When the two did arrive, they rushed into the cave and Catherine spoke right away.

"We have to get moving," she said. "I think my mom is getting suspicious. I overheard them talking about putting extra security protocols onto the time machine. They fear you and Rebecca might try to figure out how to use it. Lewis and I came here to tell you that if we go, we go tonight. Now!"

Lewis said, "Rebecca, you and Lonney get the other kids. Cath and I will set the dials of the time machine. You bring everyone to the computer room."

"Maybe you should take Lonney with you," Rebecca said. "He can help hold the adults off if they discover you. I'll get the kids and meet you there. What about Iris and Kent? Do they know? Will they come?"

"They know," said Catherine, as they all moved toward the door. "But they want to stay. They feel this place is our best chance. And we spoke to the other kids just before we met up with you—some of them want to stay, too."

"What?" said Rebecca. She couldn't believe her ears.

"That's right," repeated Catherine. "Robert and Mike want to stay. So do Sue and Blair."

"But—" objected Rebecca.

"They don't want to leave," said Catherine flatly. "They like it better here. They say they're treated well—better than at their homes—and they don't want to live through a world war. They don't think we'll be able to change anything."

"So don't waste time trying to convince them," instructed Lewis. "Just get the ones who want to come and meet us as soon as you can."

Rebecca nodded. By this time they were at the door.

Lewis pushed the button. He, Catherine, and Lonney hurried down the street, toward the computer room. Rebecca slipped away to fetch the others. She looked at her watch. It was two-thirty a.m.

She opened the door to her quarters, slipped in, made sure the door was shut behind her so no light would escape, then flicked on the light.

"Ssshhh," she whispered as the girls sat up in bed and began to talk. "Listen, we're going to have to leave *now*. Whoever is coming—get dressed as fast as you can."

"But I thought you were going to plan it," objected Blair. "I thought we'd have more time to think."

"No time," responded Rebecca. Ellen and Lindsay scrambled out of bed, grabbed their clothes from the piles beside the cots, and began to dress.

Rebecca ran over to Blair and Sue, who were still sitting on their cots. She gave them each a big hug. She didn't know what to say, for nothing seemed right. Finally she just said goodbye and turned to leave. Ellen and Lindsay also hugged the other girls.

Rebecca waited until Ellen and Lindsay joined her at the door. Then she turned out the light.

"We have to get the boys," she whispered. They sprinted down the street to the boys' sleeping quarters.

She opened the door and herded the girls in.

"Hey!" a voice called. "Who's there?"

Rebecca flipped on the light. "It's us," she said to the surprised faces. "We're leaving—now. I'll explain later. Just get dressed."

Only Nathan and Paul got out of their beds. They were dressed in minutes. Quickly, they said goodbye to Robert and Mike and wished them luck.

"Yeah, good luck to you, too," Mike replied, looking as if he was ready to cry.

Turning off the light, Rebecca opened the door, then led the kids down the side street to the main street and into the computer room. They all moved as silently as they could and they managed to reach the computer room without being seen.

When they arrived at the computer room Rebecca found Lewis at the time-machine console calling out numbers to Catherine as they checked and double-checked their figures.

They turned to Rebecca.

"We're all set," said Catherine. She looked slightly pale.

"Are you sure you want to go?" Rebecca asked.

"Yes!" Catherine said.

"Catherine, Lewis!" They could hear Laura's voice.

"She's looking for us," said Catherine. "We have to get out of here. Everyone in. One by one."

Lewis looked over the display one more time, then keyed in a final program.

"I'll fix it so no one can follow us once we're at the other end," said Lewis. "Now hurry."

One by one, the kids stepped into the glass booth. One by one, they vanished. Only Lewis, Catherine, Rebecca, and Lonney were left.

"You two go first," Rebecca commanded, "and start work on the machine at the other end."

"Lewis!" a desperate male voice called. And then Laura's voice, "Catherine!" For a moment both Lewis and Catherine froze.

"You can still stay," Rebecca said. "It's not too late."

"I hope they'll understand," said Catherine, tears in her voice, and she stepped into the machine.

Rebecca was shocked to see tears running down Lewis's face as he followed Catherine.

The voices were closer now.

Rebecca grasped Lonney's hand and together they moved into the centre of the machine.

"No!" Laura screamed, and that was the last thing Rebecca heard before she and Lonney were thrust into blackness.

CHAPTER EIGHT

Rebecca and Lonney stepped out of the glass booth. The kids were clustered around the booth except Lewis and Catherine, who were already reprogramming the time machine.

Lewis turned to the others.

"All right," he said, "we've fixed it to short circuit. It could blow up. We'd better get out of here just in case."

"There's a door at the back," Rebecca called. Lindsay ran ahead and unbolted the door. Once it was open, everyone rushed outside. There was a large, open field behind the warehouse. Rebecca and Lonney ran behind the others as they crossed the field.

"This should be far enough," said Lewis, and he sank to the ground. The others had just collapsed around him when they heard the explosion. They turned back and saw smoke and then fire billowing out of the warehouse windows.

"It'll be quite a long time before they can rebuild that machine," commented Lewis. Then he looked up at the sky. "We might never be able to go back," he said quietly.

Catherine was staring at the sky as if hypnotized. Lewis reached for her hand. He looked frightened.

"It's so big," he whispered to Catherine, gazing at the vast prairie sky.

"The pictures," said Catherine. "We've studied so many pictures and videos of the surface. But they don't do it justice, do they? It's beautiful! And the air! The smell!" She took a deep breath.

The others also took deep breaths of the cool, clean, fragrant air. Suddenly they were all fighting back tears.

"We can't let all this be destroyed," said Catherine. "We *can't.*"

"Listen." It was the first time Lonney had spoken. "I hear sirens. Someone must've heard the explosion. Let's get out of here."

"To my house," Rebecca said. "My parents will know what to do."

Rebecca led them away from the warehouse, down back lanes so the police wouldn't notice them. When they finally reached Rebecca's house, Rebecca found the door unlocked as she had left it so long ago. The group straggled in after her. She led them to the den and told them to stay there, shutting the door behind her.

Then she went into the kitchen. Empty. She peered into the dining room and noticed that the door was open to the back sunroom. She took a deep breath and walked up to the door. Her parents were eating breakfast.

"There's plenty of eggs if you want some, sweetheart," her mom said. "Better hurry, don't want to be late for your field trip."

Rebecca stared at her and at her dad.

"Were you out for an early morning ride?" he asked. "Your mom was about to get worried," he added, rolling his eyes. "I told her you'd be out on your bike."

"I've been gone forever," Rebecca said, finally finding her

voice. "I thought you'd have the police out and an Amber alert and everything."

"It's 7:30 a.m.," her dad said. "When did you leave? I'm pretty sure I heard you get up a little after six. I wouldn't call that *ages*, although your mom was getting anxious. We were both happy to hear the door open."

Rebecca realized that the time machine must have sent her back to just about the time she left. Well, that was pretty great. Her parents would have been going crazy otherwise. But Nathan, Paul and Ellen and Lindsey, and Lonney—well, their parents must surely have contacted the police by now. Or maybe not. After all, that's why they were taken—because no one would really miss them.

With that thought, she turned quickly to head back to the den. Her mom would ask a lot of questions. She'd better tell the others to get home as quick as they could.

Everyone exchanged phone numbers and then hurried on their way. That left Catherine and Lewis.

"Wait here," Rebecca instructed them. "I don't know how on earth I'm going to explain all this to my parents, but I'd better do it right away. Wish me luck."

Her mother, who taught physics at the university, and her father, a fifth grade teacher, often talked about the strange things the future could bring. But could they ever believe this? She took a deep breath. She had to try. Especially because of Catherine and Lewis.

Back in the sunroom, Rebecca told them what had happened, trying not to leave anything out. They listened in silence, often exchanging worried looks. Rebecca wondered if they thought she had lost her mind.

When she was finished, she said as convincingly as she could, "I'm not making a word of this up. You know I've never lied to you. You know I've never made up stories. And," she added, "it wasn't a dream."

Her parents didn't speak.

"Look," Rebecca continued, "Catherine and Lewis have no one here. No home. No family. I want them to stay with us. Maybe you can tell people that they're cousins of ours, that their parents died and they've come to live with us. Anything! Please, Mom. Please, Dad! They need someone to look after them."

Rebecca's father shook his head and laughed uncertainly.

"Never in all my life have I heard such a crazy story," he said. "Look, I understand that you have some friends and that they are in trouble and need a place to stay. But why the tall tale? Why not just tell us where are these kids are really from? We'll have to figure all that out eventually, Rebecca."

"Come into the den and see for yourself."

Her mom and dad followed her to the den. They were puzzled, to say the least, by Lewis and Catherine.

Catherine, Lewis, Rebecca, and her dad and her mom all stared at each other for a long awkward moment. Rebecca's stomach broke the silence with a large growl.

"Any chance of breakfast?" she asked her dad.

"Absolutely," he answered, seemingly glad of something practical to do. "What shall we have?"

"Everything!" declared Rebecca. "Oranges, waffles, eggs, cereal—"

Rebecca's mom said, "I have a meeting at nine that I can't get out of, but I'll be right back when it's done." And she gave Rebecca "the look"—the one that meant, "We're not finished by a long shot, young lady."

Soon they were all sitting at the kitchen table. Lewis and Catherine bit into everything gingerly, but they tasted it all.

Rebecca passed them each an orange. They peered at the oranges, turned them around, smelled them, but didn't have the vaguest idea what to do with them. Rebecca's dad took the oranges, cut them in four pieces, then placed the pieces in front of Catherine and Lewis. He seemed to be play-acting, as if this was some elaborate prank and he was into the spirit of it.

"Eat everything except the skin," Rebecca said.

Catherine tasted it first.

"It's so sweet!" she exclaimed. "It's, it's…oh, I can't even say…"

Lewis also seemed to have lost the words he needed to describe just how good that orange tasted.

Rebecca peeled hers, then bit into it. They were right. It was delicious, almost beyond description. How could she ever have taken something so wonderful for granted?

Next they had waffles with syrup. Rebecca was glad her mom kept lots frozen, ready to be toasted. It was Rebecca's favourite breakfast. Then eggs.

Rebecca didn't usually like eggs. But after not being able to eat them, they seemed strangely appealing. After the first bite of her fried egg, Rebecca set down her fork.

"No," she said, "I still don't like them."

Catherine looked at the egg which was staring up from her plate, and pushed the plate away.

"No, thank you," she said. "I've already eaten too much. I couldn't."

"Better take it easy," suggested Rebecca. "After eating mush all your life, real food might be hard on your stomachs."

Rebecca's dad asked her to go into the sunroom with him.

"Rebecca, I can take a joke as well as the next guy," he said. "But this has gone on long enough. There are two children here and I want to know their names and where they live, and I want to call their parents. Now."

Rebecca sat down. She was suddenly very tired. Exhausted.

"Dad, you can call the police. You can report them. You can look all over the world for their parents. But I am telling you the truth. They are from our future. They have no one here but us. If they can't come and live with us, they will be homeless, or have to go to foster homes or something."

Her dad shook his head, evidently disappointed in Rebecca's behaviour.

"Dad, I'm really, really sorry. This isn't a joke. Look, why don't you go and talk to them? Ask them anything. Anything at all. See if you still think it's a joke after that."

And he did. He sat with them in the kitchen and asked them to describe the place they lived, then shook his head again. Anyone who'd been to The Museum of Man and Nature could have described that.

He asked them to describe what they ate. Again he was

unimpressed. Anyone could come up with goo.

Rebecca could see he was becoming more unconvinced, not less.

"Let them go sit outside in the backyard," she suggested. "You and I can stay here and talk."

She took them out back and got them settled on some lawn chairs, which were placed on brick pavers, just beside the sunroom. Beside the pavers were flowerbeds. At the end of the lawn were more beds, a crab apple tree, some lilac bushes, and then the garage.

Once they were settled, she motioned for her dad to sit quietly and to listen to them talk.

The first thing Catherine said was, "Can you hear that?"

"I hear so many things," said Lewis. "But do you mean that bird singing?"

Catherine started to cry. "It's the most beautiful thing I've ever heard."

"But look at the colours," Lewis said. He was pointing to the lilies and the snap dragons.

"The pictures don't do them justice," she said. They both went over to the flowers, where they smelled them and touched them and finally sat down on the grass. Rebecca could see Catherine pick a handful of grass and bring it up to her face to feel it and to smell it.

"Very convincing acting," her dad said. "But this is just making me more angry. Why go to all this trouble to put one over on me?" he looked around suddenly for a camera. "Am I being Punked?"

"Here's the thing, Dad," said Rebecca, getting rather angry

herself. "Why would I do that to you? You know I'd never punk you. I'd never up set you up for no reason. So if this isn't a joke then maybe I'm telling you the truth."

Her dad stared at her for a moment, and then stared at Catherine and Lewis.

"But it can't…"

"It can't—but it is," Rebecca said firmly.

Her dad slumped down in his chair.

"Mom and I need to talk," he said.

"I know," said Rebecca.

CHAPTER NINE

"Hi, Lonney," said Rebecca, as the group sat down around a large picnic table at the park the next day.

Lonney flashed her a grin, obviously glad to see her.

"So now what?" Nathan said.

"What did your mom and dad say to having two new kids to take care of?" Ellen asked.

"I can tell you they still aren't totally on side," Rebecca said, "but I think they're getting there. My mom seemed to come around faster than my dad after she got back from her meeting. She asked Lewis and Catherine all these really complicated questions about science and the time machine, and she was shocked by their answers. Shocked and, I think, convinced on some level because they knew things—well, they know things that scientists here in this time don't know."

"I impressed her quite a lot, I think," said Lewis confidently.

"And so did Catherine," Rebecca said. "But look, we need to think about what to do next. We've seen what the future will be like if we don't do *something*. We have to try to change it. It's our responsibility."

"But how?" Lonney asked. "We're just kids. Nobody cares about what we think."

"Before this all started, I was doing this study on schools, as you know," Rebecca answered, flashing Lonney a smile, "and I found out there wasn't that much time given to science. Well, we can demand that teachers give us courses on nuclear energy. Everything about it—power plants, weapons, the effects of nuclear war. We need to learn about chemical and biological weapons, too. We go to about five different schools. We can all demand it."

"They'll never go for it!" said Lonney, in his old discouraged voice.

"If the schools won't offer these courses, why, we'll learn about it and spread the word ourselves," said Rebecca.

"Not only that," added Ellen. "I think we should organize rallies at the school on disarmament. Whole day events, inviting speakers, getting everyone in the school involved."

"I think we should do street theatre!" exclaimed Lindsay. "We could make up plays, wear ghastly costumes. 'Life after the Bomb!' Stuff like that! Do them in the school halls and even right downtown. How about in front of the legislature? Or City Hall?"

"What about starting our own group?" interrupted Rebecca. "We could organize everything from there."

"That would be better than doing it all in school," said Lonney. "We'll leave school and spend our time doing that."

"You can't leave school," exclaimed Catherine. "There are things you'll have to learn if you want people to listen to you."

"It's true," Rebecca agreed. "We need people to respect us and then maybe they'll listen. You know," she continued, "there's more to it than figuring out ways to get people's attention and ways to convince the world to disarm, isn't there? I mean, the first step has to be to disarm. But," she started to pace up and down, "maybe we'd better start thinking about how countries, and people, can start getting along better. Figure out ways to settle fights without going to war—"

"It's too bad," said Lewis, "that your U.N. doesn't have more power. Maybe that would be a way…Rebecca's right," he said decisively, "we have to get rid of the immediate threat, the weapons. But we have to think about the deeper problems, too, the things that *cause* war. And you'll all have to stay in school. I suppose Catherine and I will, too."

"You know," Lonney said, "while I was lying in bed this morning, I was thinking—"

"No!" laughed Rebecca, glad to be able to break the tension.

Lonney made a face at her and persisted.

"Yeah," he said, "and I was *thinking* that the five of us got kidnapped in the first place because we were hanging around the parks at weird hours. Because for one reason or another we didn't want to be home."

The others all looked at the ground. No one really wanted to talk about why they weren't happy at home.

"Yeah," he said, "we don't have to go into the reasons. But why can't we help each other out a bit?" He took a deep breath. "I mean, for me, my dad goes after me when he drinks. Well, if I see him go for the bottle, I know what'll come next. So I get out. But I have nowhere to go. What if we form sort of a club and we always make sure there's somewhere to go? Like, when my dad isn't drinking he's okay—so anyone in trouble could come to my house. A quick phone call to find out who's home and who can take you for the night, and it's goodbye parks and all the other crazy people you can meet when you're out on the street all night."

He paused again. "Well, what do you think?"

Lindsay responded. "I think it's a great idea! Just great!"

"Yeah," said Rebecca, "and there's my place too. You're all welcome to stay in my basement any time you want. Maybe it could be, like, the headquarters for our peace group. But...here's the thing," Rebecca added slowly. "At some point—maybe not today or tomorrow—you guys might need help. Like, help with that stuff at home you are coping with." She looked around. Lonney nodded. And then so did the others. It looked to Rebecca as if they all felt like they had found a new family—with each other.

And Rebecca, of course, really did have a new family. She looked at Catherine and Lewis. She would have to keep her sense of humour sharp if she and Lewis were to be brother and sister.

"Can Lonney and I talk for a minute?" she asked the others. They drifted away over to the swings.

"You know," Rebecca said to Lonney when they were alone, "last winter my dad got stuck in the lane. My mom got out and pushed, the next-door neighbour came over and pushed, but the car wouldn't budge. Then I got out. Dad sorta told me not to bother—I mean if the grownups couldn't move the car...But I pushed with them and the car rocked back and forth, back and forth, until one last big push and it was free!"

Rebecca looked away from Lonney, and stared at the dirt.

"I mean, one kid may not seem like that much but...one person does matter...and together...we could make a difference."

She stopped. Would Lonney think she was being corny or stupid?

She looked up shyly and to her surprise saw tears welling up in his eyes.

His eyes met hers.

"We can make a difference," he said. "And we will."

PART TWO

CHAPTER TEN

Rebecca couldn't believe that she had only been back from the future for a week. A week! She had spent it showing Lewis and Catherine their new world and seeing it for herself through their eyes. And she was pretty happy with it! Now she lay on her back, the high grass tickling her neck and legs. She gazed up through the deep green leaves of the maple tree to the clear blue sky. The leaves shimmered in the sunlight. She sighed with delight. There is nothing more beautiful in the whole world, she thought, than the green of the leaves and the blue of the sky, one against the other. The leaves and branches made intricate patterns against the blue. Two birds called to each other through the silence. *O-can-a. O-can-a.*

Today she and Lewis and Cath had gone with her parents to the annual picnic at Assiniboine Park. Her parents and their friends, a group that had been together since high school, assembled once every summer to eat food, run races, and pull as many muscles as possible. Naturally, "The Gang," as they affectionately called themselves, saw each other often during the year. But this was a chance to see each other's children as well.

The kids had to go, of course, and it really wasn't too bad, Rebecca admitted to herself. Except for the races. There was nothing she hated more than that awful moment between "Get set" and "Go."

Rebecca was alone in the small clearing for a few blissful minutes. Everyone else, even Lewis and Catherine, had wanted to go for ice cream. Well, especially Lewis and Catherine. They were both more than a little obsessed with food, and if her parents even hinted at any kind of treat they were first in line. Understandable. But Rebecca had begged off, craving just a few minutes of peace and quiet.

Slowly, Rebecca sat up and rested her back against the tree. Perhaps she should catch up with the others. After all, a Fudgesicle wouldn't be such a—

"Oh!" she exclaimed out loud. Standing directly in front of her, where a moment before there had been nothing, was a boy. His hair was bright red, his face an almost shocking white, his eyes a deep green. He wore a long silky top which flowed almost to his knees, the sleeves puffed around the shoulder, then tight from elbow to wrist; and silky pants which clung like tights and were tucked into soft suede silver boots. Reds, greens, blues, and yellows shot across the fabric in a jagged lightning design.

For a brief moment their eyes met—his desperate, shocked, and...was it *defiant*?—hers astonished. He opened his mouth as if to speak, then closed it, looked around, turned, and fled. Within seconds he had disappeared through the willows that surrounded the clearing.

For a moment Rebecca sat, too stunned to move. Then she jumped up. Had she imagined it? Or had someone really appeared right in front of her?

"Oh my gosh," she murmured. For again, directly in front of her, this time unmistakably coming from nowhere that she could see, was another boy. He, too, looked desperate. He had light brown hair and light brown eyes; his face was round, pleasant. His mouth was set in a determined line. His clothes were the same style as the other boy's—only the colours differed. His top was gold, the tight pants lime green. He wore gold suede boots and a lime green beret.

He looked around and blurted out, "Was there someone else here just now? Red hair, about my age…?"

"Uh, y-yes," Rebecca stammered, "Yes, I saw him. He popped up, just like you, out of nowhere. What's happening? You both just…appeared!"

"Which way did he go?" asked the boy. "I can't lose him. I can't. You must tell me!"

Rebecca pointed at the spot where she'd seen the other boy disappear.

"Thank you," called the boy over his shoulder, already running through the willows. "Thank you so much."

Rebecca stood for a moment, not moving, trying to convince herself she'd imagined the whole thing. Then her curiosity took over.

She darted through the trees. She could still see both boys. The first boy was halfway across a large grassy field; the second had only just run into the field and was only a stone's throw away from her. Rebecca, although she hated racing, always won. She suspected she could catch the boy if she wanted to. Burning with curiosity, she sprinted after the second boy. She was gaining on him rapidly when he glanced over his shoulder and saw her.

"I see him!" he called. "It's all right! I can find him, thank you!"

Rebecca just waved and smiled. She didn't stop but she slowed her pace to a jog. Polite, she thought, very polite. Nice way to say get lost, but he can't make me. I've got to find out what this is about.

Then the first boy disappeared behind some trees that Rebecca knew surrounded the duck pond. Rebecca picked up her pace and followed the second boy as he raced through to the pond area as well. There she had to pull herself up short, for just ahead, the second boy was stalking the first. The redhead was staring, as if hypnotized, at the ducks.

The other boy waited a moment, then spoke very softly: "Jonathon."

Jonathon whirled around.

"Hi," said the other boy.

"Mark!" exclaimed Jonathon, obviously shocked. "How did you find me?" He paused. "And why?"

"You can't stay here," said Mark firmly. "I've come to get you. You don't know what effect you'd have. Think about it, Jonathon. One person. Little things you do could change other little things. Those could add up to big things and then we, at home, might not even exist. Do you know how dangerous it is for you to be here unsupervised?"

Jonathon nodded his head, his eyes shining.

"Yes," he said. "I know. It's a wild chance. Maybe my being here will change everything. I know it's unlikely. But it's possible. It's *possible*. And I'm going to stay!"

Rebecca stood, listening. It sounded terrifyingly familiar.

You might change everything?

"You shouldn't have come," said Jonathon. "Now you'll have to stay, too."

"No, Jonathon," said Mark urgently. "I *don't* have to stay and neither do you. Look, I know how you feel, but—but you have to come back. You'll be lost here with no one to take care of you. It's so different here—you won't make it on your own. If we go back now, no one will know the difference. I don't think they've discovered we're missing yet. We can still go back!"

"And if they have?" asked Jonathon. "Then what? You know what'll happen to us," he said bitterly. "To both of us. Anyway," he added, looking almost cheerful for a moment, "we can't get back now. I deliberately left the transmitter behind."

Mark walked over to him and held out his hand. Cupped in the palm of his hand was a small, shiny black box. There seemed to be small red lights shining inside it.

"Wh—wh—what did you do that for?" Jonathon shouted. "You know they only have to activate that—they can trace us now—"

"But we can get back with it!" Mark countered.

Rebecca had to see that box. A *transmitter*, the redhead had said. She decided it was time for the direct approach. She walked up to the boys.

"Get away from us!" Jonathon shouted as she approached.

"Listen," Mark said to Rebecca, "please leave us alone. This is private. It's nothing to do with you. Please—"

"I'm sorry," she said, reaching out to Mark. "I'm really—"

She never got to finish her sentence. Just as her hand was

about to touch the boy's sleeve, the world seemed to go…soft. And when it solidified around her again, she was no longer in Assiniboine Park. There were no birds singing, no grass, no trees, no duck pond. For a split second she felt a gut-wrenching fear that she, too, would soften and disappear. She grabbed each of her arms with the opposite hand and hugged herself tight, as if she could hold herself together. Her eyes were seeing something, but her mind was not processing the information. She saw that she was standing with Jonathon and Mark in a small round structure, large enough across for three adults to just fit comfortably.

"Mark," cried Jonathon, tears in his eyes, "what have you done?"

Just then, part of the wall seemed to slide up and a large opening appeared. Four tall, very large men wearing shiny, black, knee-high leather boots, black shirts, and black helmets with tinted, black plastic visors stood at the opening.

"What's happened?" Rebecca cried out. "Where am I?"

She grabbed Mark's hand. "What's happened?"

He looked at her. His eyes filled with pity.

"Whoever you are," he said, "I'm sorry, I'm very sorry—"

CHAPTER ELEVEN

Rebecca was being pushed—and there was nothing Rebecca hated more than someone pushing her around.

"Stop it!" she protested. "Cut it out! You don't have to push me. I can walk!"

But the large, silent man dressed in black ignored her protests. A knot of fear had formed in the pit of her stomach and was sitting there like an iron ball. She yelled even louder because of it, trying to take some control.

"Big bully! Jerk! Get your kicks picking on people a quarter your size, do you?"

She tried to look around, get her bearings, but it was very difficult. Every time she attempted to focus on her surroundings she was roughly pushed forward again. She was inside a large building which seemed to be filled with displays behind glass. She caught a glimpse of shining cars of all vintages, and mannequins dressed in a wide range of styles. There were machines of all sorts—toasters, vacuum cleaners, food processors. An entire room was filled with computers, another with human-looking robots, ranging from the little Japanese-style ones Rebecca had seen on the news to life-size models that appeared far more sophisticated. Through these rooms, groups of children, and some adults, were being escorted by what seemed to be tour guides. Rebecca couldn't catch what was being said and was too mesmerized by the people to really care. Everyone was dressed in the most amazing clothes! Long robes, flowing pants, pleated silk shirts, hats, boots, flowers, feathers, and furs. Rebecca had never seen such a display of colour and design.

Suddenly she was outside, standing at the top of about fifty shiny, silver steps. All around her, buildings shot up into the air. Tall and needle-like, they seemed at least a hundred storeys high. Some were gold, others silver, many black. All shone with tinted glass which reflected the sun and sky.

The sky was a strange colour. It was more grey than blue, and yet there were no clouds. And the sun, although it shone in the cloudless sky, seemed dim. The air appeared clear, although it didn't have that clean, crisp prairie feel. The temperature was mild.

"Down those steps!" the guard shouted.

Rebecca glanced behind her and saw Mark and Jonathon stumbling through the wide doors, pushed by guards.

"Move! Move!"

They all ran down the stairs and were shoved into a sleek, black vehicle. It had three rows of seats. Two guards sat in the front. The children sat in the middle. The other two guards sat in the back. As soon as they were seated, shoulder straps and lap straps whirred silently into place and snapped the kids tightly against the seats. Rebecca almost jumped out of her skin, and by the startled looks on Mark's and Jonathon's faces, she knew that she wasn't just buckled in for safety. The vehicle seemed to lift slightly off the ground, then float down the street. The traffic was heavy and they moved slowly.

Stores lined the streets. People poured in and out of them, seemingly in a frantic rush. It was quiet in the vehicle; all sound was blocked out, but just outside the car windows was a jumble of colour and commotion.

Rebecca looked at Jonathon. He sat quietly, but Rebecca sensed fury seeping out of every pore.

He glared at her, then at Mark.

She turned to Mark. "Where am I? Tell me where I am!"

Mark, whose face had turned ashen, shook his head.

"You're in Winnipeg," he murmured.

"Winnipeg?" Rebecca repeated. And then she had a crazy thought. A *different* Winnipeg? Surely it wasn't possible that that little box...

"There's no way I could expect you to understand," Mark replied grimly.

"Try me!" she insisted. "I'm not as dumb as I look!"

Mark looked at her in surprise. "Most people in this situation would be in hysterics by now," he said, "or would have just passed out or something. But you're making jokes." He paused. "All right. I'll tell you." Choosing his words carefully, he said, "You've travelled. In one instant, you've travelled from your park to here."

"Here?" she exclaimed. "Where is *here*?"

"Quiet back there!" barked one of the guards. "No more talking!"

"I want to know where I am!" shouted Rebecca. "And I'll talk till someone tells me!"

She felt Mark's hand over hers. It was freezing cold.

"Later," he said quietly. "We'll talk about it later."

There was something honest in his manner, and something which told her it would be dangerous to pursue the question now. She sank back against the seat and pulled her hand away from Mark's while staring straight ahead.

Take deep breaths, she thought. *In, out, in, out.* She could feel herself relaxing just a bit.

You've been in tight spots before, she thought to herself. Just keep your head. There's an explanation for all this. And you'll soon find out—something. And don't jump to conclusions! Mom always says stick to the facts. After all, what would the odds be that you've time-travelled twice in less than a month? Really!

The vehicle slowed down in front of one of the very tall buildings which shimmered gold and seemed to narrow into a point at least a hundred storeys up. They turned into a short driveway. A large door at ground level rolled up and the vehicle floated into a white, bare room.

The door rolled down behind them and Rebecca knew by the sinking sensation in her stomach that they were in an elevator. Then, with a slight jarring motion, they came to a stop.

Snap! The belts slid away. The doors of the vehicle opened.

"Out! Out!" barked the guards.

But none of the children seemed to move fast enough, so rough hands reached in and yanked them out, one by one.

"Move," a guard bellowed at Rebecca. She tried to shake his hand off, but it clamped down heavily on her shoulder, the fingers digging into her flesh. "Move!"

Rebecca tried to get a good look at her surroundings, but

she could get only a quick impression. She seemed to be in a huge room. The walls were painted black, and she was shoved past row after row of black desks. People dressed in black sat working at shiny black computers.

She stumbled along, her guard hissing in her ear, "Move," his hand now on her back, pushing, always pushing. They reached a door, which slid open to the side as they approached. Rebecca was given one final shove. She found herself standing in a small white room. It had one black desk and one black chair in it. Soon she, Mark, and Jonathon had been hustled into a row in front of the chair. The guards stood right behind them. Rebecca felt like stepping back and giving her guard a good kick, but she tried to control herself. At least her anger over being pushed had made her forget some of her fear.

A small man with pale skin and thin grey hair came into the room and sat on the black chair. He wore a black uniform and his shirt was covered with red and gold medals.

"Do you know who I am?" the man said to them, speaking so softly they had to strain to hear him. Rebecca knew that trick. Teachers did it sometimes so the kids would really have to listen.

Mark and Jonathon shook their heads.

Rebecca stepped forward.

"I don't know who you are," she said. "I don't know where I am. I don't know anything. I want you to tell me," she continued, her voice breaking. "I want," and she paused, for tears were unexpectedly stinging her eyes. She took a deep breath. "I want to go home! Right now!"

The man looked at her coolly.

"I," he continued, as if she hadn't spoken, "am Chief of Police Lows, chief for this entire region. So. I want you to understand that your fate is in my hands. Answer me correctly and truthfully and you will feel my fairness. We won't even contemplate the results of answering with a lie. Will we?" He looked at them mildly.

To Rebecca's surprise, Jonathon stepped forward.

"It was really my fault," he said, speaking in a clear and defiant voice, looking right at the police chief.

"And you are...?" asked the chief.

"Jonathon Kobrin," he replied, "10037."

The chief tapped a few numbers into a console on his desk and suddenly a hologram appeared to his side, numbers scrolling rapidly on its surface.

"Go on, Kobrin."

"I wanted to experience the past for myself."

"The past!" Rebecca exclaimed. And then her heart sank. She had suspected, of course, but...

"The reality of what it was like to live in those days," continued Jonathon, ignoring her outburst. "Not on some controlled time trip, but...At any rate, I went, and my friend here..."

"Your name?" asked the chief, looking at Mark.

"Mark Simms, 99725," replied Mark, his voice shaking.

The chief punched in more numbers.

"And then Mark," continued Jonathon, "tried to save me. To bring me back and keep me out of trouble."

"And this person?" said the chief, looking at Rebecca.

"And she's from my trip," said Jonathon, this time looking at Rebecca with concern.

"What?" exclaimed the chief, leaping from his chair. "What do you mean she's *from your trip*?"

"She was standing with us when you brought us back," answered Jonathon. "I told her to go away, but she wouldn't listen!"

"What year was it?" the chief demanded.

"Exactly one hundred years ago today," answered Jonathon.

Rebecca gasped. One hundred years?

"Get me Lotts!" the chief barked.

A guard left. The chief paced up and down in such a fury that for a moment no one dared speak.

A young, thin man entered the room.

"Yes, sir," he said, "can I help you?"

"I want you to take this girl to the museum and send her back immediately. These boys were using the machine illegally and they brought her with them."

Lotts just stood there.

"I, I…"

"Well, what is it?" exploded the chief.

"I can't send her back just now, sir," answered Lotts. "The machine is malfunctioning at the moment, sir."

"Well, get it fixed!" hissed the chief. "No doubt they didn't work it quite correctly. I want her sent back!" he repeated to Lotts. "Now get busy. Don't worry," he said to Rebecca. "You'll be back home in no time. Just be patient for a moment while I deal with these two."

"But—" objected Rebecca.

"Quiet!"

Realizing that her fate was in this man's hands, Rebecca

decided to obey, at least for now, and to see what she could learn. The chief then got very busy scrutinizing the information which had come up on the holographic image. Rebecca could see pictures of both Mark and Jonathan and all sorts of data.

He looked at the boys; his gaze settled on Jonathon. "Had some trouble in your family, Kobrin? Not quite keeping up?"

Jonathon stared steadfastly ahead. He would not answer.

"It says here you haven't bought anything in over a month. Now, that's hardly patriotic, is it? And your sister, Tara. Mmmm. Not good at all."

"Now, you, Mark, on the other hand, seem to be fulfilling your duty well. Good family. Good purchasing history. Rash of you to go after your friend. Very rash. Nevertheless, you'll see how fair we can be. You can go."

Mark just stood there.

"What?" he whispered.

"You can go," the chief repeated. "But no talk about this— do you understand?"

At that moment, Lotts re-entered.

"What is it?" asked the chief.

"Well, sir," said Lotts, hardly able to find his voice. "Well, sir, it's the machine. Won't be fixed for twenty-four hours at least, sir. I'm sorry, sir."

The chief looked at Rebecca.

"Twenty-four hours," he muttered. "Have to put you in a cell, I suppose."

"Look," Rebecca demanded, "if I'm to be here for twenty-four hours, you have to tell me exactly what's going on!"

He studied her analytically. "You've been transported into the future. This is 40 R.C.E."

"It's 40 wh-what?" stammered Rebecca.

At this the chief actually laughed, although to Rebecca's ears it sounded more like gears grinding. "We live in the fortieth year of the Real Corporate Era. It's been just forty years since we adopted a new calendar, symbolizing a new beginning! This boy," he said, pointing to Jonathon, "was using the time machine illegally when he travelled back to your time. His friend tried to save him. And you—you were in the wrong place, at the wrong time. I just hope your absence won't have any effect on our future. Twenty-four hours," he muttered, "shouldn't be noticed much, shouldn't do any harm. I'll have to check the records. See if we can locate you, see if it could make a difference."

Rebecca felt quite giddy. For a moment she almost laughed. It seemed like some kind of a bizarre joke. Only a few weeks ago she'd been transported in a time machine into a future so deadly, so terrifying—but how could there be two futures? On the other hand, she certainly believed that time machines could and did exist. Yes, she thought, it's possible. It's all possible. This is probably all real and I'm in the future and they're going to put me in a cell! She was dying of curiosity. What a waste it would be for her to be locked away the whole time!

"You can't leave me alone in a cell after telling me you've transported me to the future!" she exclaimed. She looked around the room desperately. Her eyes lighted on Mark. And then she thought of something. He looked at her with such concern and sympathy that she found herself saying, "Let me stay with Mark until you can send me home! I'll be good and stay out of everyone's way."

The police chief seemed startled. Rebecca expected him to say no, but instead, after thinking for a moment, he agreed.

"All right," he said. "Why not? Can't see where that would do any damage to our past, as long as you stay in one place. Yes, all right. You take her home, Mark. Putting aside today's little incident, your past record indicates nothing that would make me distrust you. And even today, you did try to put things right. Take good care of her and show her how far we have come. Don't let her out of your sight though, even for a minute. Check in with me regularly." He seemed to puff up a bit with condescending pride. "I dare say you'll be *most* impressed with how we live here in the future. So much less barbaric now."

"Thank you," said Rebecca. "Thank you."

"Yes, sir, thank you, sir," said Mark. He paused. "Sir, I'm sure Jonathon didn't mean..."

"Just forget Jonathon, now," the chief interrupted. "For your own good, forget him."

The quiet menace Rebecca heard in his voice sent a shiver up and down her spine.

Mark and Rebecca were escorted out of the room by two guards. At least this time we're not being pushed, thought Rebecca.

"Goodbye," Rebecca heard Jonathon say as the door slid shut behind them. Mark winced.

Within minutes they were back in the vehicle, being transported through a city Mark called Winnipeg—but it wasn't a Winnipeg Rebecca recognized at all.

CHAPTER TWELVE

Rebecca and Mark sat quietly in the rear seat of the vehicle. Rebecca was far too busy trying to puzzle everything out to be frightened anymore. Two different futures? She simply couldn't get her head around that idea. Had the future already changed so much in just a week—and if so, how? Could she and Lonney and the others have changed things already, just by returning to their present? She glanced at Mark.

He was still pale; he sat with his head cushioned against the seat, his eyes closed.

Rebecca looked out of the window with great interest to see how her own city had changed and what it had changed into. The vehicle was moving slowly out of the shopping area and into what appeared to be a residential area.

Well, it certainly didn't look at all like River Heights where her house was—or in fact any neighbourhood that she was familiar with in the city. Each house was unique. Some were old and familiar—in shape, if not in colour—preserved from the 1950s or earlier. Others were shapes and sizes that she'd never seen in the city: triangular like teepees, small and boxy, or tall and thin.

Oak, birch, maple, and willow trees were in full leaf on boulevards and front lawns. The grass was green and flowers bloomed everywhere. The traffic began to thin out and soon they were driving down a street with houses not more than one storey high. They stopped.

The vehicle's door slid sideways. Rebecca noted that, so far, there didn't seem to be any regular hinged doors here. These ones all seemed somehow to be part of the wall, or in this case, the side of a vehicle. They just slid up or sideways, and then slid back into place when you had gone through. Rebecca wondered how they worked.

Mark climbed out.

"Come on," he said. "This is where I live."

Rebecca scrambled out after him and watched with relief as the black vehicle sped away. Then she noticed his house. It was triangle shaped and painted red.

"I like the red," Rebecca commented.

"Oh," said Mark, "colour is very important in our everyday life. I can explain more about that later. Everything inside is colour coded, too. Come in, please."

They walked down the narrow sidewalk to the triangular door. There were no steps. Mark placed his hands on a milky-white square in the centre of the door. The square glowed red. Then the door slid open.

Rebecca followed Mark into the house but was so struck by what she saw that she stopped short just inside the door.

The large front wall was windowless, but the two side walls which met at the back of the house in a point were clear from floor to ceiling. Trees and flowers were planted in perfect symmetry on the outside grounds so that Rebecca felt she was looking at a masterful, enormous piece of art. The colours and patterns were breathtaking. The wall behind her was a soft sky blue and a thick beige carpet covered the floor.

Along the glass walls ran long, low, clear sofas, with clear backs, so nothing marred the view. Rebecca walked over to one and touched it, expecting something hard like glass. But the material rippled and gave to her touch. Gingerly, she sat down. The sofa moved slightly and then formed around the contours of her body. It felt smooth and cool.

In the centre of the room was a clear, round table with four clear, round chairs. At one end of the blue front wall, next to the door, was a blue desk with a paper thin screen on it. It seemed to be floating, unattached to anything Rebecca could see. On the other side of the door there were a number of strange-looking machines. One was a tall, shiny, blue box; the other was also shiny and blue, but the box was short and square. The tall box stood on the floor, the short box on a blue counter beside it.

Mark was standing in front of the tall box. Rebecca, full of curiosity, walked over to join him. To her surprise, he spoke to the box.

"Two dinners, please, #137. And make it something a little special. I have a guest here."

"Right away, Mark," a nasal, male voice responded. "I'll just have to order from the General Store. We're all out."

Mark turned back to Rebecca. "Have a seat." He motioned to the chair and table in the centre of the room. "You are hungry, I hope?"

Rebecca shrugged, not knowing really.

"Wh-what is that?" she asked.

Mark looked at her in surprise.

"Oh, of course," he smiled. "You lived in a primitive time, didn't you? That's my fridge. It's ordering food." Mark spoke slowly, as if he were explaining something to a three-year-old.

"Each block shares an underground complex which stores food, household items, etc. A door in the floor of the fridge will open and the food will be lifted onto the shelves by a robotic arm. If it needs to be cooked, I put it in my stove." He pointed to the short square blue box.

"Your dinner is here, Mark," announced the voice in the fridge. "Tell stove it's menu #425."

"Tell stove yourself," retorted Mark. "Can't you see I have a guest? I'm busy."

"Oh, of course, Mark," replied the fridge. "I am sorry."

Mark shook his head and removed two silver trays from the fridge. He put them in the stove, and that seemed to activate the element—or whatever the lights inside it were. A strange aroma soon filled the room.

Mark opened the stove, pulled out the trays and set them on the table. He removed the shiny silver cover and steam rose into the air. Rebecca wondered why he hadn't burnt his hands taking it from the oven. She touched the lid. Cool outside, hot inside.

"TV dinners!" she exclaimed. "Well, I can get this at home."

"Uh-uh," snorted Mark. "This wasn't frozen. We get everything fresh every day. It's packaged like that so it can be cooked efficiently."

"Oh," said Rebecca. She looked at the food before her. "What is it?"

"Ah! Kelp steak, rice, and rice pudding for dessert. May as well enjoy it," he said quietly. "Soon we'll only be eating food pills."

Rebecca knew all about food pills. She started to ask him why that would be, but he interrupted her.

"What would you like to drink?"

"What do you have?" asked Rebecca, uncertainly.

"Coke?" suggested Mark.

Rebecca burst out laughing. "Some things never change, do they?" she said.

A knife and fork lay neatly in the tray on top of a serviette.

The steak was salty and fishy, the rice was rice, although it was spiced with something Rebecca couldn't identify, and the rice pudding was as delicious as any other rice pudding she'd had at home.

I just finished a huge picnic a few hours ago, she thought to herself. Why am I so hungry? But that picnic already seemed years ago.

"Where are your parents?" she asked Mark through a full mouth. "Working?"

"Yes," he nodded. "My mother commutes to Denver, my father to Paris. They're both travelling reps."

"Wow!" exclaimed Rebecca. "That's tough. Who takes care of you? A babysitter?"

"A what?" laughed Mark, genuinely amused. "A babysitter? I'm thirteen years old, hardly a baby."

"But surely you don't live here on your own, do you?" asked Rebecca, unable to imagine such a thing. After all, she had just turned twelve, and her parents still wouldn't leave her home alone overnight.

"Oh, no," laughed Mark. "I have Sam. Sam, come here, please."

A small section of the floor right beside the table slid aside, revealing a set of steps leading to a lower floor. Up these steps climbed a gleaming blue robot about the size and build of Mark.

"Hello, Mark," said Sam. "Did you have a successful day?"

"Well, Sam, I didn't get much work done this afternoon. I had a very strange experience…and she is part of it." He gestured to Rebecca. "This is Rebecca, Sam. She comes from the past. I was there."

"You were where, Mark? I didn't realize you had a history class today."

"No, Sam, I didn't. Never mind. I'll tell you later."

"And this young person is from the past?"

"Yes, Sam, she is, and we're supposed to take care of her until the time machine is fixed and she can go back."

"Of course. I'll just clean up here. Perhaps you could squeeze an hour of work in, Mark? Wouldn't do at all to fall behind now, would it?"

"No, no, it certainly wouldn't," Mark agreed. "You're quite right, Sam. Uh, Rebecca, would you mind if I did some work? It's awfully important."

"I suppose you have homework to do, just like we do. See, it's not just Coke that's the same."

"Oh no," answered Mark. "I'm not talking about school work. I mean my *job*."

"But what about school?" Rebecca asked, puzzled. "Don't you go to school?"

"Yes, of course I do," said Mark. "I go to school in the morning. And I work in the afternoons. Everyone over ten years old works. At sixteen, I'll work full time."

"What do you do?"

"Why, what almost everyone does, of course," answered Mark. "I'm a salesperson. That's what my parents do, only their company likes a personal touch—so they travel. I work for a clothing company and I sell scarves. I have to sell to as many stores as possible, and I even do individual sales. I do it all from here," he continued, pointing to the floating screen.

He sat down at the desk and began to talk to the screen, quoting numbers, names of stores, quantities and styles of product. The computer, because that's what Rebecca assumed it was, spoke back and also put the material on the screen for him to verify.

Rebecca watched without saying a word, her head spinning. She had heard her father ranting against new laws some states in the U.S. were passing to allow child labour again and how soon we'd be back to the 1900s where most children had to work to keep a family afloat. But in Canada? In Winnipeg? Was this the future for her descendants?

Mark worked for about half an hour, then stopped, got up, and stretched.

"Well, that will keep my head above water," he said, smiling broadly. "I just sold twenty thousand scarves to Continental Division 323."

"Good," said Rebecca, not really knowing what to say. She supposed it was good he was doing well, but the whole idea of him having to work was bizarre.

"It's important to keep up," said Mark. "I have to pay rent, buy food, buy new clothes every day, and new hologram vids every week."

"What?" exclaimed Rebecca. "Stop! Are you serious? New clothes every day? My mother would kill me. And why would you have to pay for rent and food? You're just a kid."

"Life is nothing like it was in your time," said Mark. "We have to buy every day. It's every citizen's duty. And we have to sell enough to make enough money so that we can buy."

"Does everyone sell?" asked Rebecca.

"Not the presidents or executives of companies," replied Mark, "but everyone else."

"Well, who makes the stuff?" asked Rebecca.

"Robots, of course," laughed Mark. "Machines. Manufacturing plants."

"Robots," mused Rebecca. "Can they do that?"

"Yes," Mark replied. "They run all the factories on their own. They even repair their own systems when they break down. Of course, people still do some of the programming, but often robots program other robots. Hey," he said, changing the subject, "want to go shopping with me? It's a beautiful day. And all the kids will be at the stores by now."

"But can't you just order everything on this computer?" asked Rebecca.

"Sure we can, but it doesn't look good on your record. You're supposed to get out, meet people, have fun. Wouldn't be good to be stuck inside all day, would it? C'mon, I'll show you."

It seemed pretty strange to Rebecca that if you didn't go out and have fun, it would be marked down on your record. She certainly didn't like the idea that every move a person made was being recorded and looked at by men like Chief Lows. Mark seemed happy and content, though, so maybe she was wrong.

What she had to worry about now was the shopping. Rebecca hated shopping, and her mother normally had to drag her to the stores when she needed new clothes.

"You'll like it here," Mark said confidently. "It's lots better than in your time."

"Uh, Mark, what about Jonathon?" said Rebecca, feeling bad that they didn't know what trouble Jonathon was in. "I guess he must be in big trouble. Why did he do what he did?"

Mark shook his head. "I don't know—really, I don't. You see, we use that time machine for controlled trips to the past. We go in history class, but always in small groups with a trained instructor. We view the world before the coming of the new era. But it can never be used the way he used it. That was very dangerous."

"Why?" asked Rebecca. "Why was it so dangerous?"

"When we use it, we're sure never to involve ourselves in any way in the time we're visiting. The instructor knows how to avoid all such situations. He or she is very carefully trained. No student is allowed to go before their eleventh birthday, so we can be sure they understand their responsibilities. But Jonathon was there on his own, with no supervision and no knowledge about how his actions would affect the future. Perhaps some little thing he did would change some other little thing and so on and so on until later the changes would be quite large. Perhaps this world wouldn't exist like this at all—and," he muttered, very much to himself, "at least we know what we're dealing with here. Who knows if a different future wouldn't be even worse."

"Even worse?" Rebecca repeated. "I thought you loved everything here."

Mark shot a quick glance at Rebecca, his soft brown eyes suddenly hard. Then he laughed. "But I do, I love it all. You must've misunderstood." And without stopping for breath, he went on. "Have you ever thought about what the future would be like?"

That question stopped Rebecca cold. She stared at Mark for a moment before she answered. What do I tell him? she thought to herself. That this isn't the first future I've seen? He's so—I don't know—like a school teacher, almost. Who knows how he'd react? Probably think I'm crazy. Rebecca decided to choose her words carefully.

"I think of the future," she said, "all the time. And I hope we can affect the future. Do you think one person, like Jonathon," or, she thought, like Lewis, Cath, or even me, "could make a big difference? Really change things?"

"Yes, I do think one person can change things," Mark replied. "The future," he continued, "is not necessarily a straight line. In fact, it's more like a fan. Picture yourself at the connecting point of a fan—where all the ribs join together. The decisions you and the people around you make will propel you along one or another of the fan's ribs. But then you arrive at another connecting point, and another. So the future is made up of countless possibilities."

Countless possibilities, thought Rebecca. What an incredible idea. If she had a time machine and programmed it for, say, 2244 she could land in thousands of endless different futures, perhaps a different one each trip.

Aloud she said, "And the things we do could eventually narrow the possibilities until finally we are in the future, or, I mean, *present*, we have created. And perhaps, what one person does would move us into one future instead of another. What an idea."

"Maybe I should have left him," mused Mark, again to himself. "Maybe...Jonathon was my best friend, but he hasn't worked for a month. Just stopped. Is that any way to behave? What if everyone did that? He can't just drop his responsibilities like that. I tried to talk to him, to tell him. But it didn't do any good. Must run in the family." Mark shook his head.

"What's going to happen to Jonathon?" asked Rebecca.

"I don't want to talk about it," Mark said, getting up in an abrupt motion, but Rebecca was sure she had seen sudden tears in his eyes.

"I'm sorry, Mark, we don't have to talk about it," she said apologetically. "Anyhow, I think what you did was great—trying to help him, going after him like that."

"But he was my best friend," answered Mark, a catch in his

voice. "What else could I do? I had to do something." He took a deep breath and shook his head. "Come on, let's go shopping."

Rebecca got up and followed Mark out the front door.

He led her around the house, down a beautiful path surrounded by flowers, into the back lane, where they climbed into a small, blue vehicle.

"This is my skimmer," Mark explained.

"You drive?" asked Rebecca, astounded.

"Of course," answered Mark, who seemed to have become more cheerful at the prospect of going shopping. "Everyone over ten owns and drives their own skimmer. That way more people buy vehicles. I buy a new one every six months. But by the time I'm twenty, I'll buy a new skimmer every week!"

"What do you do with the old ones?" asked Rebecca. "And your old clothes and stuff?"

Mark pointed to a small silver booth. Each house in the lane had one. To Rebecca it looked like a solid silver phone booth set neatly beside the carport, right where the garbage cans would be if this were her present. "It's a disintegrator," he said and laughed. "Don't walk into it by mistake!"

And with that, he activated the computer. The skimmer lifted off the ground, and they floated down the street.

CHAPTER THIRTEEN

"The first thing we have to do," answered Mark, "is buy you some clothes. You'll stand out like a freak in that outfit. It's so plain."

Rebecca glanced down at her shorts and t-shirt. She looked at Mark's gold silk top, his green pants, and his suede boots.

"Yeah," she sighed, "I see what you mean. But I have no money."

"Never mind," said Mark. "After the sale I just made I can afford to buy one extra outfit. And it'll look good on my record. Two outfits in one day!"

"Your record?" said Rebecca.

She was just about to ask Mark to explain how these records worked when Mark, glancing at the dash, exclaimed, "Oh, no! We forgot to check in!"

Quickly he pressed a small button on his dashboard. A voice spoke.

"Operator."

"Operator," said Mark, "please connect me with Chief of Police Lows. He's expecting me."

"One moment please."

"99725?"

"Hello, sir."

"What are you doing now, Mark?"

"We're going shopping, sir."

"Good, Mark, good. And Mark?"

"Yes, sir?"

"Don't forget to check in often. I want to know where you are at all times. I may have to bring you in quickly."

"Yes, sir. I will, sir."

"That's all. Sign off."

"Yes, sir. Signing off."

Mark turned to Rebecca with a weak smile. "That was close."

Rebecca looked at him quizzically.

"Would it really have mattered if you'd forgotten to report in?"

Mark laughed nervously.

"Of course it would! They don't tolerate mistakes or tardiness."

"They?"

"Yes, you know, the police, the Company. Look over there. We're going to that shopping centre."

Traffic was quite heavy now, and they moved slowly toward a large vehicle park.

"Ah, we're in luck," Mark said, as he manoeuvred his skimmer into a just-emptied space. The skimmer sank to the ground and the doors opened.

"C'mon," he urged. "We'll get you something really beautiful."

Rebecca and Mark walked through the lines of skimmers, across the smooth white surface of the vehicle park. People, all flamboyantly dressed, were hurrying into the shopping centre or rushing back to their skimmers, laden with parcels. Rebecca looked with interest at the large, round, smooth white building with a green domed roof. As she and Mark approached the building, a door large enough for ten shoppers to enter at the same time slid up and open.

"Wow!" Rebecca said aloud as she and Mark walked through the door.

The area inside the building was the size of a football field and was filled with light and colour. Fountains shot up into the air. The water was coloured, so the air was awash in liquid rainbows. Surrounding the fountains were exotic trees. Some of them Rebecca could identify—orange, apple, lemon, and grapefruit grew beside olive and cork trees. Palms swayed in a light breeze. Orchids, tiger lilies, mums, and roses grew out of the cropped, green grass that covered the floor. And throughout this maze of colour and fragrance were hundreds of mannequins, each one dressed in a different, elaborate outfit.

The mannequins were arranged in various postures—some leaning casually against a tree, some poised as if they were about to run or dive or throw a ball, some picking flowers, others in conversation with each other. They looked so real it was hard to tell the mannequins from the shoppers.

Rebecca stood just inside the door, staggered by the sight.

Mark laughed. "Come! Pick any outfit you want. I'll buy it for you!"

Rebecca wandered through the building with Mark, but she had a hard time concentrating on shopping. The trees, flowers, and fountains were so beautiful.

"How," she asked, "can a cork tree grow beside a fir? They need such different climates."

"They're all genetically engineered to grow under just these conditions," explained Mark. "The flowers, too, of course. Everything here is for sale," he chattered. "There's big business in landscaping. People have to change their flowers and trees at least once a month."

Rebecca stopped and stared at him.

"How can you change a tree?"

"Oh, it's easy," Mark answered. "We have machines that do all that, and special fertilizers that make the trees and flowers take immediately to their surroundings. I mean, you can't have a tree hanging around for hundreds of years. Or flowers regenerating every year. Where's the profit in that? Now choose an outfit. All the clothes are on the mannequins," Mark explained. "Find an outfit you like, then I'll show you how to order it."

"I like that top," said Rebecca, pointing to a bright red top which covered purple pants and gold lamée boots.

"You can't just get the top," Mark said. "All or nothing— even the boots are included."

"But that's not fair," Rebecca objected. "I only want the top. I'll find a different pair of pants."

"It's not a matter of fairness," Mark explained, stopping for a moment to deliver a small lecture. "It's a matter of profit. If you like the top, you have to buy the whole outfit. That way you spend more money and it's better for everyone. You can always switch and wear it with a different pair of pants at home."

"Well, I think I'll pass on that one," said Rebecca, making a face. "Red and purple? Lame."

The next one she saw was a brilliant orange top with short sleeves and short lime green pants.

"This is lovely," Mark suggested.

"No." Rebecca shook her head.

She stopped in front of a mannequin leaning gracefully against a lemon tree. It wore a pale yellow silk blouse with three-quarter sleeves which puffed just under the elbow. The blouse reached to just above the knee. There were soft yellow silk pants, which were worn tight and tucked into short silver boots. A rainbow-coloured scarf was wound around the waist.

"That one," said Rebecca. "Please." And she had to admit to herself that although she normally hated shopping, this was not so bad. In fact, she couldn't wait to try on that outfit. It really was spectacular.

Mark pressed some buttons on a small machine which had been built into the mannequin's palm and within minutes a silver robot appeared, bearing a box with her clothes in it.

"How do I know they'll fit?"

"Oh, they'll fit. Your size and measurements were taken the minute you walked through that door. Hey! There are some kids from my class at school! That robot will take you to the changing rooms. You get changed and come back out here and I'll introduce you."

The robot slid silently over the floor, weaving in and out among shoppers and displays with no effort. Rebecca hurried after it. In the centre of a cluster of giant apple trees was a small square structure covered in vines and ivy. A number of square pieces were leafless, and one of these slid up as the robot approached. The robot entered. Rebecca followed. They were in a large room, large enough for ten people to change in. Mirrors covered the walls from floor to ceiling. The floor was covered in thick purple carpet. Plush purple armchairs were placed carefully in the corners. The robot deposited the box on a long, translucent purple table, then turned and left. The door slid shut. She was alone.

Rebecca walked over to one of the chairs and sank down into it. She opened the box and stared at the clothes. She picked them up, touched them. They felt like nothing she had ever felt before. The silk was so fine, so pure, so smooth. The colour was the same shade as the sun. Slowly, almost reluctantly, she took off her own clothes, her only link with her world. Soft, cotton underwear and socks, all in yellow, lay on top of the silk shirt. She put these on first. Then the pants, the shirt, the boots.

She wound the scarf around her waist and tied it in a knot at the front, the way she'd seen it done on the mannequin. She stared at herself in the mirror. The material felt heavenly, smooth and cool against her skin. It was real, very real, and for the first time since the park, she actually believed it was happening; she had landed, for the second time, in the future. And, she thought, in some ways it was quite a nice future.

I've never been one for lots of clothes and things but everything here is so gorgeous, she thought. I don't suppose it hurts to live in this kind of…sumptuousness. Yes, that seemed the right word. It was *sumptuous*.

Now how was she to get out of the dressing room? She walked to the door and, fortunately, it slid up and out of her way.

The robot was waiting for her. It took her back to Mark and his friends. She had forgotten all about her old clothes and they remained in the changing room.

She was introduced to three kids, two boys and a girl. Mark told them she was a visitor from out of town.

They chattered on and on about their purchases and the new styles being introduced this week. Finally one of them asked where Jonathon was.

Mark shrugged.

The three kids glanced at each other and then shrugged, too, as if silently agreeing not to mention Jonathon again.

I know he was probably rotten, thought Rebecca, but if they were his friends, it's pretty strange they don't seem to care much about what's happening to him.

Mark decided it was time to leave and do some more shopping. They went back to Mark's skimmer and Mark took Rebecca downtown to a dizzying round of shops. He bought two lighting fixtures, a chair, two hologram games, and a painting. Art work, too, he explained, had to be replaced, although you could keep a painting for as long as three weeks if you really liked it.

"Surely paintings don't go into the disintegrator, too?" asked Rebecca incredulously.

"Of course," answered Mark. "Everything does. Otherwise we wouldn't need more of them, would we?"

All the shops were beautiful. It seemed to Rebecca that they used everything—fabrics, plants, stained glass—to enhance the pleasure of buying.

They were just walking out of a robot store where Mark had been showing Rebecca all the latest models, when Rebecca saw a hand catch Mark's shoulder. She turned at the same time as Mark. The girl they saw was tall, about Rebecca's age. She had long, shocking red hair, deep blue eyes, and pale white skin.

"Where is he?"

"I don't know," muttered Mark, looking down.

"Mark, you're his best friend," she implored. "He's been taken, hasn't he? Cut loose? If you won't help him, who will? Please, tell me!" Tears sparkled in her eyes.

Mark shook his head, in a stubborn gesture. "Forget it, Tara, forget it. Or your whole family will end up the same."

Then he grabbed Rebecca's hand and pulled her away. Rebecca looked back over her shoulder to see Tara standing helplessly in the middle of the street, people jostling her every which way.

"Who was that?" she asked Mark as they hurried to the skimmer.

"Mark's sister, and if she doesn't watch it, she'll end up the same as he has. I don't even want to be seen with her anymore. Contact with that family will go down badly on my record—I can see that now. I'll have to stop talking to her."

"But surely," Rebecca objected, "talking to someone can't hurt you. I mean…"

"Oh, please be quiet, Rebecca. We have to go back and check in. Hurry up."

Rebecca looked at Mark closely. A queer feeling was

beginning in the pit of her stomach. She liked Mark. And she'd assumed that Jonathon must be a real troublemaker. But was it that simple?

Back in the skimmer Mark called in. The machine was still malfunctioning. They were ordered to get some rest and check in the next morning.

They had eaten lunch late, at about two, so for dinner they just had kelp sandwiches and tofu cakes. Rebecca hated tofu so she skipped that. As they were sitting at the table, Rebecca asked, "Does Jonathon's family live around here?"

"Yes, unfortunately," sighed Mark. "It'll be hard to avoid Tara. They live just four houses down the street. But it doesn't matter. I'm never going to visit that house again."

"But Mark, why not? I still don't understand. And what has happened to Jonathon? Does he have a lawyer to help him? Maybe you should at least make sure he has a good lawyer."

Mark stared at Rebecca as if she was talking in a foreign tongue.

"A lawyer," he repeated pensively. Then he shook his head. "Rebecca, I think I'd better tell you a little bit about 40 R.C.E. It is very different from your time. I know. I've been there, in history class: the world on the brink of nuclear disaster, small wars everywhere leading to mass starvation, terrorism, crime, gangs, violence, unemployment and poverty...Well, look around you. We live in a paradise by comparison. For example, there is no war because there are no countries left to fight each other—"

"What?" exclaimed Rebecca. "What happened to Canada? That police chief said this was Winnipeg!"

"Oh, yes," said Mark. "The cities still have the same names, but we all live and work for Zanu. Everyone in the world does!"

"Zanu," repeated Rebecca. "Everyone in the world. I don't understand. What is Zanu? Like the United Nations?"

Mark laughed. "No," he snorted, "Zanu is not like the UN—that bunch of incompetents. Zanu is a corporation. The only one left."

"A corporation? But how…?"

"In your time, corporations began to move jobs to countries where labour was cheap. The corporations grew bigger, more profitable and more powerful, as countries grew poorer and weaker. Finally, corporations merged with each other until there were only three or four giant ones in the world, and then Zanu became the one and only corporation.

"Zanu labs produce medicines. Zanu mines the oceans for food and minerals, it builds our houses, it…well, it takes care of us. So there's no more crime, or poverty, or any of those awful problems you had in your time—and believe me, those problems only got worse—especially poverty because very few people could get jobs. But here, as long as everybody works hard and sells and contributes, it can keep on forever. Can you imagine what would happen if all of a sudden no one wanted to sell? Or consume? Everything would fall apart. There'd be chaos. Maybe even war, like in the past."

"And Jonathon wasn't buying. That's what the chief said…" Rebecca murmured. She was astonished. An entire world—one big business.

"Yes," exclaimed Mark, "and if everyone stopped buying, it would be *terrible*. The whole system would collapse. We'd

110

starve, we'd die. You see, we all have to be responsible. We have to keep buying."

"Well," said Rebecca, "I see what you mean. Still," she said, "you'd think there'd be a little room for someone who feels differently—like, can't work, or loves to study instead."

"No," said Mark. "Not unless we want chaos."

With that he got up from the table.

"C'mon. I'll show you where you'll sleep tonight."

And that was the end of the discussion.

CHAPTER FOURTEEN

Mark stepped on a small red button on the floor and a square slid away, revealing a stairway.

"This way," he said. They walked down about ten carpet-covered steps. A hallway ran the length of the house, narrowing until both sides joined to form a door at the end. Directly to Rebecca's right was a door, and to the left was another one.

"This is my parents' room," Mark said, indicating one on the left. Then he pressed a small red button beside the door to the right. The door slid sideways and Mark walked in. "You can sleep in here."

Rebecca followed him into another smaller, triangular room. The long side was the side with the door. There was a single bed in the front of the room. The long wall opposite, which slanted to a point at the back, was covered with mirrors. Beside the door on the left was a long, low, clear pink vanity table; beside the door on the right was a silver rack with clothes hanging on it.

Mark pointed to the small red button just inside the room, on the wall beside the door. "Press this to open the door," he instructed. He looked over the rack of clothes, which was so full he could barely see what was there, and took down a long, shocking pink silk nightdress. "It'll be big," he said, "but you'll manage, I'm sure. The bathroom is at the end of the hall. My room is across the hall—should you need anything, just let me know. I'll wake you in the morning. Have a good rest. Good night."

"Good night," replied Rebecca.

Mark smiled at Rebecca and walked out the door and across the hall to his room. Rebecca pressed the red button, and the door slid closed. She looked around. The bed was covered in a bright pink satin cover, the floor carpeted in pale mauve. She inspected the vanity table. It was full of bottles, jars, tubes. She picked one up. " 'Younga' skin cream for men," the label said. She picked up a tube and opened it. White lipstick. She opened a jar labelled "Devastation." A very strong perfume. There were also cosmetics, deodorant, and coloured hair spray. She went over and looked at the clothes. She knew she shouldn't be snooping, but she couldn't help it. There were pants, blouses, suits, evening gowns, and about fifty different pairs of boots and shoes. There was so much of everything: it was all so beautiful, so lavish, so—enthralling. But it almost made her dizzy. It seemed to her that after a while, you would want more and more and more and more until you could think of nothing else.

She changed into the nightgown and lay down between the cool, pale pink, silk sheets, her head sinking into the floral-patterned pillows.

But Rebecca couldn't sleep. She tossed and turned. Her mind was racing. A whole world run by one company. It was hard to believe. Certainly, even in her time, a lot of people thought business could solve the world's problems. The most important leaders in the West had thought so for a long time now. Her class studied the newspapers for ten minutes every day, so she knew a bit about it. And if it was the answer to war, disease, poverty—well, could it be wrong?

Still, the image of Tara, standing in the middle of the street, haunted her. Of course, there would always be people who wanted to wreck everything...maybe Jonathon and Tara were like that. But why did something in the pit of her stomach feel... well...

Oh, I can't stand this, she thought, and she got out of bed. She put on her new clothes, then pressed the button to the bedroom door. It slid open. She climbed the stairs, the door sliding open as she reached the first floor. The large inner room was now dark, crowded with shapes and shadows. In fact, one shadow was moving toward her!

"Mark?" she asked tentatively.

"It is Sam," said the robot. "Is there something I can do for you?"

"Uh, no, Sam, I just can't sleep. Maybe some fresh air would help."

"But it is very late and you are not allowed on the streets after 12 o'clock."

"Oh, all right, Sam. I won't go on the street. I'll stay in the front yard or right in front of the door, if that makes you happy."

"Happy?" asked Sam. "It will not make me happy or unhappy. But yes, if you stay by the door I suppose that will be satisfactory."

"Thanks, Sam. Could you turn on a small lamp for me? Just so I can find the door?"

Sam did so and Rebecca crossed the room, pushed the

button for the front door, and let herself out into the night.

The temperature hadn't changed since the afternoon. The air was the same, too. It didn't have that fresh night smell. But there was a faint smell of flowers.

Rebecca sat down on the grass and looked up at the sky. At home there was nothing she found more wonderful than sitting in her yard, looking up at the sky filled with stars. She'd find all the constellations she knew, make wishes, and drink in the beauty and peace of a still, clear night. But much to her surprise, here she could see no stars. There had been no clouds earlier. She sighed. She was beginning to feel homesick. What about her parents? They'd be frantic with worry. What would they have thought when they got back from getting ice cream, and she was gone?

A dull, humming sound broke through her thoughts, disturbing the otherwise quiet night. A skimmer was driving slowly along the street, headlights dimmed. It passed her and continued down the street. Rebecca got up and crossed the lawn so she could see where the skimmer was going. She stood behind a large oak tree and watched. It was so dark that it was hard to tell what was happening. The skimmer stopped along the curb. She saw four large shapes get out of it. They moved up to one of the houses. She could hear a pounding on the door. It slid open and light momentarily flooded the scene.

She saw four police guards, all dressed in black, weapons drawn, standing at the door. She gasped. Then she saw a man and woman step out of the house. They looked frightened. The woman was objecting, pointing back to the house. One of the police shook his head and roughly pushed the couple toward the skimmer. And then

Rebecca saw Tara standing in the doorway and heard the woman call, "Go back in dear, please. Be good, don't worry. We'll be back soon!"

Tara cried out, "Mother! Father!" The girl made a movement as if to follow them but stopped when a police officer turned and pointed a weapon directly at her.

Tara backed into the house and the door closed.

Blackness once again enveloped the scene, as if a TV had suddenly shorted out. Rebecca saw the skimmer drive off.

She waited until it had completely disappeared into the blackness and then, without stopping to think about what she was doing, she ran, heart pounding, to Tara's house. She knocked softly on the door, looking around, afraid someone might be watching.

The door slid open. For a moment Tara was speechless.

"Wh—wh—who are you?" she stammered, her face streaked with tears. She seemed confused by Rebecca's presence. "I thought you were…Who are you?"

"You thought it was the police again," said Rebecca. She looked at Tara's desolate expression and a rush of pity swept over her. "I saw the whole thing. Look, let me in. I don't want to be seen."

Tara stepped aside and let Rebecca in.

Rebecca looked around. They were in a house very much like Mark's. "Is anyone else here?" she asked.

Tara shook her head. She was shaking.

"Well, *I* don't even know what I'm doing here," said Rebecca, suddenly realizing it herself. "It's just—I saw everything and—I don't know, I thought maybe you'd need help."

"Who are you?" repeated Tara, staring at Rebecca in bewilderment.

"Oh, I'm sorry. You don't remember me, do you? I was with Mark this afternoon when you stopped him. I guess you didn't really notice me..."

"No," said Tara. "I guess I didn't. I was thinking about something else."

"Yeah," said Rebecca, "I know. Look, you'd better sit down. You look awful. Do you have a blanket or something?"

Tara pointed to a long, low, beige sofa which ran along one wall. On it was a black silk shawl with white fringes. Rebecca guided Tara to the sofa, wrapped her in the shawl, then sat her down. Rebecca sat down beside her. Tara sat hunched over on the sofa. She couldn't stop shaking.

"Tell me why they took your parents," said Rebecca. "I really want to know. And why did Jonathon do what he did?"

"What do you know about Jonathon?" asked Tara, sitting up straight. "Do you know something?"

Rebecca shook her head. "Not much. But I'm not from here, exactly. Not from Zanu."

"You're not?" Tara seemed to become even more confused.

"No," said Rebecca, "I definitely am not. My name is Rebecca, and..."

"Just a minute," whispered Tara. She pointed at the computer console in the centre of the room.

"They can tune in on us whenever they want," Tara whispered, practically in Rebecca's ear, "and they might very well want to see if I do anything or contact anyone now that my parents are gone. Don't say anything more. If you aren't from

117

Zanu, you probably shouldn't be here. You'll get in trouble if they hear you."

"How about outside?" whispered Rebecca. "Can they hear out there?"

Tara shook her head.

Rebecca motioned to Tara to turn off all the lights. Tara did so and they quietly let themselves out into the black night. Tara took Rebecca's hand and led her into the backyard. They crouched underneath a gigantic weeping willow.

"Look," Rebecca continued to whisper, "I might be able to tell you something about Jonathon, but first, you tell me what happened just now."

"You saw," answered Tara, her tears returning. "They came and took my parents."

"But where," asked Rebecca, "and why? And what will happen to them?"

"Why should I trust you?" asked Tara. "Why should I tell you? I don't know anything about you."

"Okay," sighed Rebecca. "I'll trust you first."

In spite of what Mark had said, Rebecca liked Tara and trusted her immediately. She began with her first glimpse of Jonathon as he appeared in the park and ended with the evening's police raid on Tara's house.

"It's unbelievable," Tara whispered shakily to Rebecca, the shawl still pulled tightly around her. "So you really come from our past?"

"Really," said Rebecca.

"But you seem like anyone else," said Tara. "I thought

anyone from before R.C.E. would be...I don't know...well, sort of primitive. After all, look at the conditions you lived in."

Rebecca laughed. "It's not that long ago! We're not exactly Neanderthals—although, on second thought, if you saw some of the kids in my class..." She giggled. Much to her surprise, Tara giggled, too.

"Yes," Tara said, "I know what you mean."

"Anyway," said Rebecca, "Mark seems to think you've got things pretty good here—although I sure don't like those police. Why did Jonathon do what he did if it was so dangerous?"

Once again, Tara sighed. "I don't know if it's because they took Laura, or if he would have done it anyway."

"Laura?"

"My older sister." Tara's voice was so low Rebecca could hardly catch the words. "She was supposed to leave school to work full time. But she wanted to stay in school! She wanted to study history. So they came to get her. They told us she would stay in school but a different kind of school. 'Re-education' they called it. She'd learn what her real duties were—duties to Zanu. Then they'd let her come back. That was over a month ago. We haven't heard from her since.

"Then Jonathon, well, he just didn't fit. He liked to write stories and draw. And he used to do that instead of working. He didn't pay much attention in school when he was being taught about Zanu. Instead, he'd daydream, draw...I don't know. He hated shopping, he hated selling. He got hold of all sorts of books from the past—illegally. Books we aren't allowed to read. He'd swipe the microchips from the history museum, then put them back before anyone realized they were gone. He would take incredible risks. He could've been caught anytime. I know he didn't like the world before Zanu. But he didn't like this one either. He always talked to me about being free—about having the right to live any way you wanted to. And you know," said Tara, her voice dropping even lower, if that was possible, "I agree with him. It's true, we don't want war and crime and disease. But that doesn't mean we have to have *this*. Anyone who doesn't behave correctly just gets taken away. It's not right. I'm sure it isn't."

Now Rebecca knew why she'd felt uncomfortable with some of the things Mark had told her. Zanu had created a peaceful world, but at what price?

"You're right," she said to Tara. "Peace shouldn't mean that you have to give up being free. It shouldn't! But where do they take the people they arrest? Do you have any idea? And why did they take your parents?"

"My parents started asking questions about Laura and now about Jonathon. They couldn't just sit by and let them disappear like that!" Tara paused. "I don't know where Zanu takes them. Jonathon always thought it was up north somewhere where it's cold and snowy, or to such an isolated, lonely place that no guards or police would be needed. And of course, even if someone did escape and make it back to civilization, they'd be picked up again the second they set foot in the city."

"Why would they get caught so easily?"

"There's a force field around the city. All travel is strictly controlled by Zanu."

Rebecca began to realize how powerful Zanu really was—and that she was in a very precarious situation.

"Look, Tara," she said, "if what you say about Zanu is true, I'd better get back to Mark's. If they're watching everything, they might know I'm not there. And," she added, "I want to help you, but I also want to get back to my home and to my time. In fact, maybe there's something I can do! Maybe I could tell the police chief that I won't go home unless he frees your family. He knows he has to send me back—he said something about not messing up this present. Anyway, we'll think of something!"

She squeezed Tara's hand in encouragement. They walked to the front of the house. Tara was just about to go in when Rebecca grabbed her arm.

"Uh oh," Rebecca whispered. "There's a skimmer in front of Mark's house! Wait here, I'm going to try to get closer and see if I can find out what's going on."

Rebecca ran from tree to tree, grateful for the complete blackness that surrounded her. Finally, she scurried under a large fir just beside Mark's house.

The police guards were talking to Mark in his doorway.

"We picked up a communication," one of them said, "from Kobrin's, twenty minutes ago. We were sure she would be back here by now. She must be found and brought to the police centre. The chief told me personally that when they checked her file, it read that she mysteriously disappeared on July 3. She was never seen or heard from again. It was assumed that she was kidnapped and murdered. We cannot let her return to the past now because somehow that could change our present. She must be found. If she turns up, call us immediately. We will search Kobrin's house and grounds. The Kobrin girl will also have to be taken in." And they turned to the police vehicle.

Rebecca, her heart pounding so hard she was sure they could hear it, turned and scrambled back to the place where Tara was waiting. She reached her just before the police skimmer pulled up to the Kobrins' house.

"C'mon," she said, grabbing Tara's hand, pulling her toward the lane. "They're after us both!"

CHAPTER FIFTEEN

"Quick," said Tara, "my skimmer."

They ran as fast as they could to the back lane and climbed into the skimmer. Tara pushed some controls, the skimmer lifted off, and they drove down the back lane with their lights out.

"Where can we go?" asked Rebecca. "Is there anywhere we can hide?"

"I don't know, I can't think!" cried Tara. "I don't know anyone who could hide us…"

She was driving very fast. Up and down lanes. "Well, let's get out of the city then. We can hide in the country 'til we figure out something."

"No, there's a force field. We can't get out."

"There must be somewhere we can go!"

Tara was crying. "There isn't. There isn't. They'll catch us. They have GPS, satellites, drones. All kinds of things. They'll track us down in no time."

"What about friends? You must have friends who would help hide you."

"Hide us from Zanu?" wailed Tara. "We'd just get my friends in trouble."

"Tara!" commanded Rebecca. "Pull yourself together! Think!"

Tara took some deep, gulping breaths. The skimmer continued to speed up and down dark lanes.

In the silence, Rebecca could feel her heart pounding. Her hands had turned to ice. She realized she was in the worst danger she could possibly be in. Presumed dead. Murdered. Never returned. The words echoed in her head. If Zanu captured her, they'd never return her to her own time. In fact, they would probably kill her to make sure she would never go home. Tara continued to let out big gulping sobs.

"Stop it!" Rebecca said, as firmly as she could. "This has to stop. We have to be calm. If they catch us, we have to be ready and alert. A chance may come to escape at any point. We have to be ready to take it. If we're shivering messes, we've already given up."

Tara looked at her. Rebecca's firmness and conviction startled her into silence. She took a deep breath.

"I'm sorry," she sniffed, "you're right, of course. I'll try. I'll try." She paused. "Maybe there *is* someone…"

"Really? Who?" urged Rebecca.

"Someone Jonathan mentioned, then Mother."

"Who? Where are they?"

"They live near the outskirts of the city," said Tara. "4430-564 Street. Mother made me memorize it. But what if we get them in trouble?"

"We won't drive up to their front door!" exclaimed Rebecca. "We'll park the skimmer a little way from the house—we'll sneak up."

"Oh! Look!" cried Tara. "A guard skim." Up ahead, passing along a cross street, a pair of lights flashed and was gone.

Tara backed her skimmer up and programmed the computer to take them at top speed to their destination. It only took a few minutes to get there. Tara drove past the house. Then they drove to the end of the block and stopped the skimmer.

Suddenly, seemingly out of nowhere, lights of a guard skimmer drew up in front of them, blocking the girls' way. A second skimmer boxed them in from behind. They were trapped!

"Isn't there any way out?" Rebecca cried. "Make a break for it, Tara. Drive through them! They'll kill us anyway!" But Tara seemed frozen by fear and didn't respond.

The two pairs of guards leapt out of their skimmers, weapons drawn and aimed at the girls' heads. As they approached Tara's skimmer, they motioned for Rebecca and Tara to get out.

But before Tara could release the doors, a flash of light zapped across the blackness and the two guards on her side of the skimmer slumped to the ground. Rebecca watched as the same thing happened on her side. Within seconds, a young woman and a young man were tapping on their windows. Tara stared at the one by her window but didn't move.

"Tara!" hissed Rebecca. "Roll down the windows! These people want to talk to us!"

As if she were a robot obeying orders, Tara pressed the window control.

"You must leave the city," the young woman on Tara's side whispered hoarsely as soon as the window was open. "In exactly ten minutes, there will be a force field open at these co-ordinates."

She handed Tara a slip of paper. "Feed that into your computer. Be there."

125

The young man handed Rebecca a small, black triangular object. "This is a jamming device." He pressed a small button. The object glowed a faint red. "It is now activated. It will jam all frequencies. Once you are clear of the city, you must try to find others who have been cut loose. It's your only hope. This is all we can do. Now go!"

"Good luck," whispered the woman, and they both disappeared into the night. Tara sat immobile.

"Tara," said Rebecca, reaching over and shaking her. "Feed that into your computer. Now! We have ten minutes. Get us out of here!"

"But…" Tara was still dazed.

"Never mind them! Can you feed the directions into your computer?"

Tara looked at the piece of paper for a moment—which seemed like an eternity to Rebecca—then nodded. The dash computer was lit up so that one could easily program it, even at night. Tara, her hands shaking so much she could barely push the right numbers, fed the information into the computer.

"It's done," she said.

"Then let's go!" Rebecca commanded.

Tara nodded again. She raised the skimmer above the level of the other two, and they sped away.

"Who on earth were those people?" asked Rebecca. "They appeared right out of nowhere…"

"And how did they know we would be there, needing help?" added Tara, her voice still weak.

"Good question," mused Rebecca. "The only other person

who knew we were missing and in trouble was…Mark. That policeman told Mark." She paused and looked at Tara. "But would *Mark*? No, he would have helped Zanu catch us, I think. Or…"

It was too confusing. She couldn't think straight. And she knew they weren't out of danger. Even if by some miracle they did get out of the city, how would they find other people who could help them? And how, *how,* could she ever get back to that time machine and home again?

"We're approaching the force field," announced Tara. The skimmer drew up in front of a faint, shimmering, white glow which seemed to extend as far as the eye could see, both to the right and to the left, as well as from the ground up. They could see nothing through it. They waited then, each thinking—but afraid to say it—that they might be too late. Suddenly, a black hole opened right in front of them, pushing aside the light.

"Go! Go!" Rebecca urged. "Tara!"

Tara hesitated and looked at Rebecca. "Maybe it's better to be captured. We'll be alone out there. I'm scared."

"Tara," pleaded Rebecca, "I'm scared, too. But it's our only real chance. Being caught is no chance at all."

Tara paused for a split second before she pushed the button. This time Rebecca watched what she did. It had occurred to her that she might have to take over the skimmer if anything happened to Tara.

Rebecca could feel a pull on the skimmer as it approached the black hole, then it shuddered as it pushed against an invisible force. She shuddered too, wondering if the vehicle would disinte-grate under the stress of the force field and if she and Tara would be destroyed along with it. But in the next instant, the skimmer bolted like a horse set free and shot away from the force field into an all-encompassing blackness.

CHAPTER SIXTEEN

It was black. A blackness so complete it was overwhelming. A nightmare-like nothingness. There were no stars, no moon, no haze from city or town lights. The little light beams the skimmer emitted seemed to be swallowed up the moment they left their source.

Tara raised the skimmer to its highest level in order to avoid any obstacles which might be there, and they flew like a low-flying airplane over the land.

Rebecca had never experienced such emptiness, such blackness, before. Both she and Tara were quiet, staring into the dizzying space around them. Rebecca felt lost—completely and totally lost. Where were they going? North? What would they find? Other people? Could you live out here? Was it dangerous? Were there bears or wolves? Could they make a fire? Would they survive? She was frightened. Very frightened.

She wasn't alone though. She looked at Tara. How would Tara manage out here? Perhaps she would just give up and die. Tara's eyes were closed and she seemed to be half asleep. It was so quiet. The skimmer hummed on, a gentle vibration lulling them both...Rebecca's eyes began to close, despite her effort to watch for something—anything—any break in the dark.

Rebecca sat up with a jolt. Sunlight was streaming into the skimmer. Tara was fast asleep beside her.

Rebecca looked at her watch. It was 5:30 a.m. She felt groggy, disoriented. How could they have fallen asleep? Perhaps it was the shock.

Rebecca looked around and down. They were flying over a small lake surrounded by forest. The conifers were brown on the tops and on one side. Must be the windward side, Rebecca thought. Still, Rebecca had seen that on the way to Falcon Lake in the summer, so this discolouration was already happening in her time. The leaves of the other trees—birches, and oaks mainly—also had a yellowish brown hue, not the rich green she so loved at this time of year—and that was new to her. There was no sign of life anywhere.

But then something caught her attention.

"Tara! Tara! Wake up! I see something! No, I see somebody. I mean *somebodies*. I see people!"

Tara opened her eyes and sat bolt upright. A look of terror swept over her face.

"Oh, I'm sorry I frightened you, Tara. It's just—we just passed over some people." Rebecca turned her head to look through the back window, hoping to pick out some landmarks to help remember where she had spotted them.

Tara looked at Rebecca and then looked around. She seemed bewildered. "But where are we? What is all that?" She pointed below them.

"Well, I don't know where we are," Rebecca answered, still craned around, looking back. "But I saw some people. Turn this thing

130

around so we can find them again. If we go much farther, we'll lose them."

"But," objected Tara, "we don't know who they are. If they were cut loose they could be criminals, or... or..."

"Tara! Come on! You were cut loose, and your parents and your sister and probably Jonathon—and you're hardly criminals. Who knows—it may be some of your family down there!"

Tara turned the skimmer around and headed back the way they'd come. The people were grouped at the far end of the lake. They were huddled together, sleeping under the trees. Just beside them, right at the water's edge, there was a natural clearing. Tara set the skimmer down. By the time they were on the ground all the people had awakened and were sitting up, watching the girls' skimmer. Tara leaned forward, frowning, as she looked through the windshield, then shook her head.

"No one I know," she sighed.

It was a small group—six people. There were two elderly people—a man and a woman—two women who looked as if they were in their twenties, a tall, lanky boy somewhere in his teens, and a very young boy.

"Look at that little boy!" exclaimed Rebecca. "What could he possibly have done to end up here?"

They all looked drawn and pale, their cheeks sunken, their eyes dull. Their once-beautiful clothes were only tatters now, which they gathered around themselves.

The tall, lanky boy stepped forward. His legs seemed to give way beneath him for a moment, but with obvious effort he pulled himself up straight and walked toward the skimmer.

"C'mon," said Rebecca, "open the doors. I want to talk to them."

Tara, with obvious reluctance, pressed the button and the doors opened. Rebecca climbed out. Her bones cracked and she realized her neck and back hurt from sleeping upright for hours. The early morning chill bit through her thin clothes, and she shivered. She managed a tentative smile as she approached the young man and said, "Hi!"

"Hello," he responded, with a smile that was quite dazzling in its openness and warmth. Now that she saw him closer, she thought he looked about fifteen or sixteen years old. He had large brown eyes in a long face, and long, brown hair which was tangled and looked like it hadn't been washed for weeks.

"Dare I ask," he continued, "how on earth you got here?"

"In this, of course," replied Rebecca, turning toward the skimmer.

Tara got out of the skimmer and came around to stand beside Rebecca. The cool air seemed to shock her and she wrapped her arms around herself. She began to shiver.

"Yes," he said, "I can see that, but how on earth did you get out in a skimmer? And who are you? You seem too young to be Zanu guards."

Rebecca grimaced. "We're not Zanu guards," she said with disgust. "We're being chased by them, in fact. We got into this skimmer and tried to escape, but they caught us, and then suddenly we were rescued by some strangers. They told us how to escape the force field—and here we are."

The young man nodded. He looked very solemn. "That's

good, very good. It means they're getting organized—you won't be the last they'll help."

"Who?" asked Rebecca. "Who were they?"

"Oh," he laughed, "I don't know their names, but I do know that there's a group of people who are working together against Zanu. They want to return the world to democracy. A true democracy. A world government where each of us gets an equal vote."

"Oh," breathed Rebecca, "so they are like an underground movement."

"Yes," he said, "that's what it is, a resistance."

"Excuse me," Tara interrupted, "but what are you doing here?"

The young man looked at her. "Well," he said, a faint smile on his face, "I believe we're dying."

Tara blanched.

"I'm sorry to alarm you," he said, "I'd like to put a better light on it—and now that you've arrived there might be hope."

He stopped and his face seemed to brighten, "Maybe we could use the skimmer somehow..."

While he was talking, the others had begun to gather round the skimmer.

The small boy walked up to Tara and Rebecca. He was thin, with blond curly hair, blue eyes, and pale skin which was blistered and red from the sun.

"What's your names?" the boy asked, looking up at Tara and Rebecca, grabbing the bottom of Tara's shirt in his little fist.

Tara managed a smile and crouched down to his level. "My name is Tara," she replied, "and this is my friend Rebecca. What's your name?"

"Paul," he said, "and I'm very bad."

"Are you, Paul?" asked Tara.

"Oh, yes!" declared. Paul. "I don't like to buy new toys, I like my old ones. I won't throw them in the dis-ina-mator, I won't! And I won't go shopping with Mommy and Daddy. I lie on the ground and scream and scream. And," he said, his eyes growing very wide, "I smashed our computer into bits."

Rebecca listened in amazement.

"And they sent you here—because of that?"

Paul nodded and tried to look brave.

"Where are your Mommy and Daddy?" asked Tara.

"At home," the boy whispered, as he fought back tears.

Tara put her arms around him and hugged him. Paul started to pull away, but then climbed into her lap and wrapped his arms around her neck.

They were very near the shore of the lake, the trees just a few yards behind them. They were standing on a dull, brown gravel surface, which changed to sand nearer the water. The few scraggly bushes growing just behind the gravel were stunted and yellowish. The forest also looked thinned out, sparse.

"Ouch!" yelped Tara, swatting her neck.

"What is it? What's the matter?" asked Rebecca.

"I don't know. My neck, it hurts. Ouch!" she exclaimed again.

Suddenly Rebecca slapped her cheek and inspected her hand.

"Oh, Tara," she moaned, "it's mosquitoes, and probably black flies if it really hurts."

"And horseflies and wasps. All sorts of mean creatures," laughed the young man. He had a wonderful, infectious laugh.

"We're probably the first food they've had in a long time. Most of the animals seem to be gone. Oh," he said, "excuse me, please meet the others." He held out his arm toward the elderly couple. "This is Sonya and David." Then he indicated the two young women. "Kristin and Rachel, and you've met Paul."

"And you?" asked Rebecca.

"Oh, I'm Michael."

"Don't you have any shelter here?" asked Rebecca, looking around.

"No shelter," replied Michael blithely, "no food. And the water is undrinkable."

"You can't drink the water?" Rebecca said with dismay. "Why not?" Suddenly she felt terribly hungry and terribly thirsty.

"It's polluted," said David, his voice flat and bitter. "It's dead and rotten, like everything around us. A wasteland."

"But," objected Rebecca, "it's not possible! Why, I've travelled up north; it's beautiful, it's not dead. There are tons of animals. The water has algae in it, but I mean, you just boil it and…"

Rebecca realized they were all looking at her very strangely.

"You'd better explain," suggested Tara. "They don't know what you're talking about."

"Well," said Rebecca, "I'm from the past."

"What?" laughed Michael. "That's a good joke."

"It's no joke," Rebecca said patiently. "I wish it was. Do you want to hear the whole story?"

"Absolutely," stated Michael, and he got everyone to sit down around Rebecca. As briefly as she could, she told them of her journey from another time.

"Wow!" Michael said, when she'd finished. "There are so many questions I'd like to ask you."

"Yes, well, there're some really important questions I need to ask you," said Rebecca. "Why did those people send us out of the city? There's nothing out here. Nothing. Why couldn't they have helped us hide in the city? And," she paused and looked around, "why is there nothing out here? I don't understand. Why is it a wasteland? It used to be so beautiful. You could fish, swim, drink the water—as long as it was boiled. What happened?"

"I told you," replied David, "pollution. When the big corporations took over, they cared more about making money than about anything else. They got around the pollution controls and environmental standards. *Deregulation* was the buzz word—they called regulation a job killer. They polluted the air and the water and now you can see the result. And," he added, "the force field around the city is not just to control the population—the UV levels are so high that people get sick if they aren't in the protected bubble, and the air quality is so poor that no one can live out here for long."

"And as to your first question," Michael interrupted, "we can only guess why they sent you out here. Before I was cut loose, there was talk among some of us about setting up a network in the north, a base we could work from, and a place to send people who were cut loose. They must've hoped that you'd find some people, like us, and we'd use the skimmer. They may also have been afraid you'd be caught in the city. Now we can use this skimmer. This could be just the chance we've been waiting for."

"But how can you set up anything here?" asked Rebecca.

"If it's truly a wasteland, no one can survive here. What do you eat and drink?" She paused and looked at the group. "How long have you been here?"

"They dumped us out here five days ago," answered Michael. "This is our sixth. They gave us enough water to last six days. Enough food pills to last three days."

Rebecca looked at him in disbelief. "But why...I don't understand...why not just shoot you? I mean, why the charade? Water for a week...?" She looked around at the gaunt faces. "It's a slow death. It's torture!"

"I'm afraid you've answered your own question," David replied.

"No," she shook her head, "I can't believe it. Why would they want to torture people? What would they get out of it?"

"We may learn the answer to that question any time now," answered David, his voice grim.

"Yes." Rachel spoke for the first time. "They said they'd return in six days."

"Then we'd better get away, fast!" cried Tara, jumping up and grabbing Rebecca's sleeve.

"No. No, wait!" Michael said. "You can't go. Not now. We can hide you in the forest until they're gone. If they kill us, at least you'll know what happens out here. You can warn others."

"What's the use of that?" cried Tara. "Why warn them? Where can they go? No food, no shelter, no water purifiers anywhere..."

"I don't know," Michael persisted, "but maybe we can discover something about their reasons, their plans. Stay. Please. I think there's a slim chance we can put you and your skimmer to some use. I just need some time to think..."

"Michael," interrupted Rachel, "shouldn't we get them hidden if they're going to stay?"

"Yes, of course." He looked at Rebecca and Tara. Tara was still clutching Rebecca's sleeve, poised to run.

"Will you stay?"

"I think we should, Tara," said Rebecca. "We'll be no good out there in the wilderness on our own. Michael's right. Here, with the skimmer, we might be of use."

Tara dropped Rebecca's sleeve. "I suppose you're right," she said, reluctantly.

"Come on then," said Michael. "We'll move you into the forest, out of sight. Keep your jamming device on so their scanners can't find you. And we'll have to cover the skimmer somehow as well. May I drive?" he asked Tara politely.

"Yes," she replied, smiling in spite of her anxiety, at his kind and pleasant manner.

"I'm getting to know the woods quite well," he remarked, climbing into the skimmer. "I think I can manoeuvre it into a large clump of bush about half a mile in."

Rebecca, Tara, and Paul got into the skimmer with him, Tara in front, Rebecca and Paul in the rear.

Michael started the skimmer and eased it into the forest, curving around trees and bushes, keeping it slightly above the ground and rock of the forest floor.

Eventually he stopped by a large clump of bushes.

Rebecca, Tara, and Paul climbed out and looked around. Rebecca studied the bushes. They were about three feet high, and the branches were slender. They could probably be bent, she thought.

"If we can somehow make a hole, that skimmer could just sit inside there." He looked at the bushes. "I'm going to try to force a hole into that bush by moving the skimmer forward very slowly."

He got back into the skimmer and began to nudge the bushes. Some simply cracked and broke, while others bent as if they had little life left in them. Once the skimmer was well within the bush, they all worked together to cover it.

Rebecca was astounded at just how brittle and fragile the branches were. It was terrifying to think of an entire world slowly dying. She thought of the beauty and the strength of the trees from her time—but then again, she remembered the huge stretches of brown, dying leaves on the windward side of the forest on the way to Falcon Lake. Her mouth felt dry. She was scared. Was her world dying around her, and she just hadn't realized just how bad things had become?

CHAPTER SEVENTEEN

"You'd better get back into the skimmer," Michael said to Rebecca and Tara. "We don't want them scanning two unidentified bodies. I'll be back as soon as I know something." He paused. "But if I'm not back by nightfall, you'd best come and have a look. Come on, Paul. And Paul, not a word to the guards about our new friends, all right? This will just be our little secret."

Paul nodded his head earnestly and took Michael's hand. Together they walked away into the forest, back the way they'd come.

"C'mon," said Rebecca to Tara, "let's get in. They could arrive any time." The girls bent the bushes back and squeezed into the skimmer. They sank into the plush seats. Then they heard, through the unnatural quiet of the forest, a distinctly man-made sound. It was a low hum. They could see nothing, however, through their cover.

"Must be an air machine," said Tara. "Do you think they can image us from the sky?" she added.

"Probably," answered Rebecca. "But why would they be looking for us here?"

Tara shrugged. They both lapsed into silence. The silence stretched out and out and out until—"Oh!" Tara exclaimed.

Michael was tapping on the window. Quickly Tara opened it. "What's happened?" she asked.

"They've come and gone," said Michael, looking quite grim. "But they'll be back. Come out of there. We have to talk."

The girls scrambled out of the skimmer and out from under the bushes they'd covered it with. Michael sat down and leaned against a tree. Rebecca could see that he was exhausted and weak from too much walking. He held out a small flask. "Water. They left us some." He handed it to Tara. She gulped it down.

"Go easy," he cautioned. "You may need some later."

Tara blushed and passed the flask to Rebecca. She took three large gulps, then made herself stop and offered the flask to Michael. She had never realized how wonderful cool water could be. It was the best taste in the world.

He shook his head. "You keep it. If you agree with my plan, I won't need it. They're keeping us alive for a very good reason. Information."

"Information?" asked Tara.

"You mean," asked Rebecca, "information as in *informers*?" Michael looked into her eyes, appreciating her quickness.

"Right," he nodded. "We supply them with names of people in the city who are possible malcontents and they rescue us. They take us to the Zanu headquarters on an island not far from here, feed us, care for us, then let us live in a supervised camp, well taken care of."

"That's awful," murmured Rebecca. "But it would be hard to refuse them."

"Harder and harder," Michael agreed, "as the days go by and

you know you'll die if you refuse and you get sick from drinking the water and need medical attention. Oh yes, they're clever."

"What's your plan?" asked Rebecca.

"I'll tell them I'm ready to give names. I'll go with them. Then I'll be in the compound. All the food and supplies we need are there. If I can locate them, maybe you and your skimmer can get close enough so that I can get some out—and then we can really set up a hideout."

Now it was Rebecca's turn to be scared.

"You know, Michael," she said, her voice a little high and thin, "if they catch me, they'll kill me."

"I know, Rebecca, and I don't want that to happen—not only because I don't want you hurt, but because somehow we have to get you back to your time alive. If we can do that, this present might never happen. From what you say, according to Zanu records, you're not supposed to return to your time."

"That's true," Rebecca agreed.

"So maybe just sending you back would be enough to change our present."

"Well," agreed Rebecca, "that's what that police guard seemed to be saying. That's why they don't want to send me back."

"So, we have to get you back. And," he continued, "letting you starve to death out here is not going to get you back. My plan may be dangerous, but it's no more dangerous than waiting here dying a slow death. It may be quicker there, that's all. Let's go and face it, at least! And it just might work."

Rebecca looked at him. He was right. She couldn't argue with his logic.

Suddenly, Tara spoke up. "I want to go, too. I'm not going to sit here all alone and die of starvation!"

"Of course you have to go," smiled Michael. "Who else would drive the skimmer?"

Tara responded with a wan smile.

"They'll be back shortly," said Michael, "to see which of us has broken. We've decided that both Rachel and I should go. The others are too weak to do anything once they get there."

"When should we come?" asked Rebecca.

"Tonight," replied Michael. "After midnight. We'll try to leave a sign, or watch for you, or something. If we can. Tara, I'll program your skimmer computer with the correct cordinates to get you there. We passed it on the way here so I have a pretty good idea of where it is."

Michael forced himself up and went to program the computer. Rebecca and Tara looked into each other's eyes.

"At least it's a chance, Tara," Rebecca said.

"I know," Tara agreed as she swatted a mosquito on her leg and then lowered her eyes to the ground to make sure no other strange insect was about to crawl on her. "I just wish I were home."

So do I, thought Rebecca.

After a few moments Michael emerged from the skimmer.

"I have to get back," he said. He took their hands. "Good luck," he smiled. "Don't look so gloomy. We'll be in and out of there in no time!" He gave their hands a squeeze, winked, and hurried off.

Rebecca and Tara looked at each other. Rebecca wiped her forehead. It was still morning, but it was already very hot. A black fly buzzed around her head.

"Let's wait in the skimmer," she suggested. "At least the bugs won't eat us up."

Tara nodded and they climbed into the skimmer to wait the interminable wait until nightfall.

CHAPTER EIGHTEEN

Rebecca and Tara listened to the sound of the air machine. They heard it arrive then leave again.

"I don't want to sit here all day, do you?" said Rebecca. She could usually sit for hours reading a good book or watching a movie, but now Rebecca found her legs twitching. She felt restless and anxious. She tried not to think about the night to come, but it was almost impossible not to.

"Let's go talk to the others while we wait," she said finally. "At least we can try to keep our minds busy. And," she added, "I've got lots of questions I want answered."

They found the small group resting under some birch trees. Paul was sleeping, his head on Sonya's lap. She also had her eyes closed and seemed to be asleep. David and Kristen were staring into the distance.

"Oh, hello!" they said when they saw the girls approaching.

"Hi!" said Rebecca. "May we sit with you awhile?"

David looked gravely at Rebecca. "Of course, my dear," he said. "Sit down. It's not often we get to talk to someone from our very own past."

"Oh, yes," said Kristen, as the girls settled themselves into the meagre shade of the birch trees. "Please tell us what it was like to actually live back then. From what we've seen on our school trips, it looked like a terribly dangerous world."

Rebecca couldn't keep herself from snorting, "Not like yours, you mean?"

Kristen smiled back. She was a tall young woman with long black hair and large grey eyes. "I suppose," she sighed, "the world has always been a rather dangerous place."

"It has," Rebecca agreed. "I'm in a group that is working to get the world to disarm—to be nuclear free. And there's poverty in the world—in Winnipeg, too. But there is a good side—I go to school and I don't have to work. I am free to say what I want, and when I'm eighteen, I can vote. "

"You know," David said, "big business already ran much of your so-called democracy even then. You were just unaware of it."

"What do you mean?" asked Rebecca.

"I mean," said David, "big corporations used all their money and influence to determine who really had the power. Every schoolchild here is taught how Zanu began. Because big business was so powerful, governments couldn't really stop them from doing just as they pleased. In fact, the so-called governments actually supported and defended—even covered up for—big corporations. Well, at that time they changed their names from "corporations" to "job creators" so people would see them in a better light. Of course the jobs *were* created—but not in Winnipeg, or Canada, or even the United States, but in poor countries where they could pay much less in wages and make bigger profits. And at some point, corporations were given the status of people in the law so they could give as much money as they wanted to candidates running for elected office. And who won those races? The candidates backed by the corporations!

And it was those elected officials who eventually voted to give away all the powers of the state to the corporations instead.

"At any rate, when governments became weak and ineffective the corporations got most regulations aimed at environmental safety removed." He gestured around them. "The resulting pollution from various nuclear accidents, offshore drilling, coal plants, and other irresponsible policies is still very much with us."

"I find it hard to believe," Rebecca objected, "that pollution could change things so much."

"Most certainly," said David. "Climate change—what you used to call global warming—has taken a terrible toll."

"Yes, we've studied that in school," said Rebecca. "Too much carbon dioxide in the atmosphere makes a sort of blanket of gas around the earth. The sun can get in but the heat can't get out, so the temperature of the earth rises."

"That's correct," David nodded. "Carbon dioxide, chlorofluorocarbons, methane, nitrous oxide. These substances accumulated in the atmosphere and trapped heat—what we called 'the greenhouse effect.' It developed rapidly once they started cutting down the South American rain forests. Without the trees to utilize the carbon dioxide, it just stayed in the atmosphere—in huge quantities. The prairies are now a dust bowl, the lakes are evaporating—or being drained for water, which we purify. The seas are polluted, the coral reefs decimated. The Polar and glacial ice caps melted, and that produced huge floods. New York is all underwater now. When they used to use the term global warming it gave people a false sense of what might happen—people didn't realize that suddenly an area could be hit with a record two hundred tornadoes in one day—up from a high of forty—or that extreme heat could kill so many, or that wars would result when clean water became scarce. People just thought maybe the world would get a bit warmer!"

Rebecca sank back against the tree.

"But," she said, "your world seemed like such a good place when I first got here—no disease, no wars, lots of gorgeous clothes and stuff for everybody..."

"I remember voting in the last election before Zanu took control," said David wistfully. "I was thirty then. Working as a computer programmer. I liked my job, except that I had to go where they told me to go, train where they wanted me to train, do what they wanted me to do. But I had no choice—I had to live, to eat. With the unemployment that started in 2008 we had to hang onto our jobs. No one dared complain. We were glad to be working. Governments were being "realistic" and "responsible," trying to reduce deficits and cutting back on aid to the poor. You had to work to live. What choice did we have?" He shook his head.

"There are always choices."

Rebecca turned to see who was contradicting David. It was the older woman, Sonya. "We could have fought them. We could have been more concerned while we had the chance to change things. It would have been better than this—and perhaps this never would have happened. There were people then who screamed as loud as they could not to cut programs but to grow them, to let governments stimulate the economy and to create

148

jobs, building roads and bridges and houses. They were drowned out by the big money of the corporations. But never mind," she said, smiling at Rebecca, "we'll get you back alive. I'm sure of it. And then, maybe we'll get another chance."

"A chance to follow another rib of the fan," said Rebecca.

"What?" asked David.

But his voice began to sound far away. It was so hot. Kristen was asking Tara about her family. Rebecca's eyes grew heavy. The air shimmered around her. She lay down on the ground and closed her eyes, listening to Tara talk about her sister and brother. And before she knew it, she was asleep.

When she woke it was still light. Her throat was so parched she couldn't swallow. She sat up. Everyone around her was asleep, sprawled out on the ground under the trees, except Paul, who was splashing in the water of the lake. She looked at him dreamily. It looked so wonderful, so cool. Maybe she'd join him. She reached over and took a small sip of the water in her flask. That was better. At least she could swallow now, and then the thought hit her.

"Paul!" she screamed, leaping up, "Paul, come out of there! Paul!" She felt herself running, running. But it was too late. When she got to the edge of the lake she could see him ducking under, swallowing water, splashing. "Oh, Paul!" she cried, "come out. That water's bad. You mustn't swallow it. Come out, please!"

"No!" he yelled. "Don't want to. Want to watch me swim?" He dog-paddled a bit. "My mommy taught me!"

"Paul!" Rebecca commanded, putting on her sternest babysitter voice. "You come out this minute or you'll be in big trouble."

Paul looked at her doubtfully for a moment, then smiled.

"I don't care," he said. "I'm always in big trouble."

Tara was standing beside Rebecca now. The others were all awake, watching. Paul looked at Tara.

"Want to come in, Tara?"

"No, Paul, I can't," she answered. "But Paul, come here for a minute. I have to tell you something."

Reluctantly, Paul splashed to the sandy edge of the lake.

"What?" he asked suspiciously.

"You know," she said, "Rebecca and I have to go away tonight. And when we come back, there's one thing I'd like better than anything in the whole world."

"What?" Paul asked, his suspicion giving way to curiosity.

"A little brother."

"Really?" asked Paul, looking up into Tara's eyes. Then he was distracted by a horsefly which started to circle around and around his head. He tried to hit it, but couldn't. Finally it flew off to bother Rebecca.

"Yes," Tara answered, when she had his attention again, "really. All my family is gone, just like yours, and well, I thought maybe we could be a family, just you and me."

He looked at her seriously for a moment, considering her words.

"All right," he answered finally.

"Good," sighed Tara in relief.

Paul turned and splashed back into the water up to his waist.

"No, wait," she called to him, "don't go back in there. If

150

you're to be my family you have to stay healthy. And you might get sick if you swim in the water. So come out now. I want a good, strong, healthy brother."

Paul turned back and looked at Tara. He looked at the water. He smacked the water with the palm of his hand and watched until the concentric circles he had produced had faded away. He sighed, then he walked out, digging his feet into the sandy bottom of the lake to slow his progress as much as possible. Tara bent down and picked him up. He wrapped his arms around her.

Rebecca, Paul, and Tara walked back under the trees. Finally the sun began to set.

"I think it's time," Rebecca said. "We should get back to the skimmer while there's still some light."

Paul threw his arms around Tara and clung to her. Rebecca could see his little body shivering.

"He's burning," Tara said to Rebecca, holding him close.

"My tummy hurts," Paul complained.

"Don't worry, Paul," Tara whispered in his ear. "We'll bring food and water and some medicine to make your tummy better."

"I hate medicine!"

Tara laughed. "I know. I hate it, too."

"Now be a good boy," Rebecca said in a stern voice. "No more swimming in the lake. Okay?" She ruffled his hair with her hand.

Kristen had to pull Paul off Tara's neck. Rebecca and Tara said goodbye to the others, then turned and hurried into the forest. It was still very hot and the mosquitoes were terrible. Tara, in her short pants and sleeveless top, was covered in bites. They were even biting Rebecca through her thin silk clothes. Rebecca and Tara ran scrambling over dead branches, their boots sinking slightly into a layer of dead, reddish-brown pine needles which carpeted the forest floor. Soon they were at the skimmer. They leapt in, shutting out most of the bugs. Tara manoeuvred the skimmer out of the bush and into a small clearing.

Again they had to wait. They occupied their time by killing all the mosquitoes in the skimmer. Finally, the sun set. Clouds scudded across the sky, and a full moon peeked through when it could.

Rebecca looked at her watch. 11:45 p.m.

"Let's go," she said to Tara.

Tara started the skimmer. It lifted straight up out of the trees. Then she instructed the computer to follow the coordinates Michael had fed into it earlier that day. The skimmer turned slightly, then raced over the trees. They were on their way to Zanu headquarters.

CHAPTER NINETEEN

"This is crazy," muttered Rebecca. "We're not sure where they are, or anything!"

"We know they're on an island and we have to land away from the complex," said Tara, sounding almost calm.

Rebecca looked at her in surprise.

"Aren't you scared?" she said.

Tara managed a weak smile. "Yes," she said, "I'm terrified. But I don't know...seeing Paul so helpless there, and thinking about my family and about what Sonya said—well, we have a real chance to help now. I'm going to try my best. And," she murmured, "maybe they have medicine there. Paul is going to need medicine. I don't think his body is strong enough to fight without help."

Rebecca took a deep breath. If Tara could pull herself together, then so could she.

A strong wind was picking up and the small skimmer began to shake. It tilted to one side, straightened out with a bump, then tilted to the other side.

"There it is!" exclaimed Rebecca as the skimmer straightened out again. Lights blinked at them out of the darkness. They were flying across water and hadn't realized it because the moon was covered by clouds. "Can you see anywhere to land?"

"I'll put it down as close to the water as possible," said Tara. "I can't tell how much land there is on the other side of the buildings, but jammer or no jammer, I don't want to fly right over them."

"No," shuddered Rebecca, "they would just have to look up to see us."

Tara put the skimmer down near the water's edge. They were close enough to the lighted buildings to see them through the thin forest and bush.

Tara moved the skimmer right up to the tree line and then manoeuvred in between two thin trees.

"That's good enough," said Rebecca. "We want to be able to get out fast and it'll take us too long to try to get further into the forest. Let's go!"

They jumped out of the skimmer and began their cautious trek toward the Zanu headquarters by the light of the moon. The wind blew strong and hot at their backs. The air had barely cooled off at all. They were both drenched with sweat.

As they came to the edge of the bush, they could see a huge structure immediately in front of them. It was so bright because of the moonlight that both girls had to shield their eyes. The entire structure, a huge triangle, was made of reflecting glass.

Rebecca squinted, trying to see more. There seemed to be two more large triangles attached to the one in front of them, but they angled away in such a manner as to suggest a semi-circle of larger triangles.

To Rebecca they looked like giant, modern pyramids, all glaring light and glass. She thought they were at least ten storeys high. As she studied them, looking for a way in, a black oval, just the size of a door, appeared in the glittering wall directly in front of them. Catching Tara's hand, Rebecca ran toward the opening, not knowing whether she would find a Zanu guard or Michael. They were almost at the door when a cloud covered the moon. They could see nothing. They couldn't even tell how far they were from the building or where exactly the opening was. With one hand Rebecca clutched Tara's hand so hard that Tara gave a little yelp. Her other hand was extended, groping for the door. They inched forward. All was black.

Suddenly she and Tara were gripped, together, in a big bear hug. A familiar voice whispered, "See, told you it would be easy."

Michael grabbed each of them by the hand. "This way, and be quiet. This is the prisoners' sleeping quarters. And I can tell you, the people here have already denounced their best friends. They'd turn us in without a second thought."

"Where's Rachel?" whispered Rebecca.

"She's gone ahead to the supply section to see what she can find. Now," he said, whispering so quietly they could barely hear him, "we're in a passageway which leads from the sleeping quarters into the living quarters. That's the big central triangle. This whole compound is a circle of triangles, each one serving a different function. From the living quarters we'll go through the interrogation centre and into the supply section. Beside the supply triangle are the guards' sleeping quarters, then their living quarters, then the stores, and the baths. In the centre of the circle are all their air machines, out in the open. I'm telling you all this in case we get separated. Nowhere is safe, but security is pretty lax because they don't think they have anything or anyone to worry about. All right, let's not keep Rachel waiting. I'll lead the way. Keep one hand on me, the other on the wall."

Rebecca grabbed the back of Michael's shirt, while Tara clutched the back of Rebecca's top. The passageway was narrow, so they walked in single file. It was slow going because the passage was pitch black, except for the occasional tiny blue button which glowed out of the darkness on the walls.

Michael stopped short. A small red button gleamed in the dark. He pressed it and silently a door slid open. They passed through. He pressed another red button on the other side. The door slid shut. Again they walked on, feeling their way through the dark in absolute silence.

They passed through another door, then another. Finally, Michael opened the door to a huge space, brightly lit. Yellow polystyrene boxes filled the entire space, row on row, right up to the ceiling. It looked, at first glance, as if they were all suspended in mid-air, but then Rebecca noticed the clear plastic shelves, extending from wall to wall, supporting them. A computer console stood in the centre of the shiny yellow floor. Large robot arms dangled from the shelves, looking like free-floating limbs. One was lowering a box to where Rachel stood, waiting. She turned as she heard them enter.

"Oh," she sighed with relief, "you made it! I've collected a year's supply of water-purifying agents and a year's supply of food pills. And that box has medicines in it."

They saw two large boxes sitting on the floor beside her. The robot arm placed the third box at her feet. She pulled open the flaps and then nodded to the others. "Antibiotics, anti-viral drugs, and antiseptics."

"All right," said Michael, "we've got everything. Now let's get out of here."

"Wait! What's that?" said Tara in a terrified whisper.

They could hear the sound of boots coming down the corridor, closer and closer.

"Hide!" ordered Rachel.

Each of them grabbed a box and dragged it behind the closest line of boxes. Then they ran toward the side walls of the large room. The door opened. They all fell flat where they were.

"What's the light doing on in here?" barked an angry voice.

"Probably Duncan again," responded another voice, this one gruff, tired. "Always trying to make more work for us. As if I don't have enough on my hands—you, you get all the fun work."

"Yeah," laughed the first, "I just sit back and let them babble away into the recorder. I can't complain. But don't think I didn't have to work my way up. I had a full year of disintegrator duty before I got this posting."

"I can't stand listening to all that wailing and moaning," replied the second voice. " 'But you said we'd be taken care of!' Some of them fall down, kiss my boot. I zap 'em right away then. Can't stand it. Throw 'em in already dead. 'I *am* taking care of you!' I say." The voice laughed.

Shivers ran up and down Rebecca's spine.

"We better have a look around here," said the first voice. "Just to make sure...Hey, look at this! The computer's on. Come on—up and down every row."

It was finished. Rebecca sighed. She felt strangely calm now, although her heart was pounding so loudly she could barely hear. They had tried their best—it was all they could have done.

"Don't shoot!" a voice rang out. It was Rachel. She was walking forward, right up to the guards.

"What're you doing in here?" barked one of the guards.

"Exploring," she replied, flippantly.

"A comedian! We have a comedian here!" said the first voice. "Well, let's see how funny you are in the interrogation unit. March!"

The lights went off, the door slid shut, and the guards' boots could be heard echoing down the hallway. No one moved until it was silent again. Then Rebecca heard a series of thuds and bumps and after a moment of fright, realized it must be Michael, trying to find the light switch. Finally the lights came back on. Rebecca and Tara stood up, tried to pick up their boxes, but finding them quite heavy, gave up and dragged them toward the door. Michael did the same.

"There must be weapons in here somewhere," Michael said to them, scanning the rows and rows of identical, yellow boxes. "They'll kill her in there, I know they will. We've got to try to get her out."

"But what about the others?" Tara objected. "We could all get caught trying to rescue her—then what?"

Michael looked at Rebecca. "In your day, your vote would be the tie-breaker."

Rebecca looked at them both. Her heart was still pounding from their close call. They had almost been caught. If it hadn't been for Rachel's courage they certainly would have been. Rachel wouldn't want them to come after her. She'd want them to try to escape, to help the others.

How could Rebecca choose?

She bent over and scratched a particularly itchy mosquito bite on her ankle. She thought about what could be happening to Rachel. By the time she straightened up, she'd made up her mind.

"I can't stand the thought of them hurting her. Let's try to get her out."

Michael nodded, his face taking on the look of grim determination. "Good! But we'll need some help." He ran to the computer and punched in the information he wanted. The screen displayed where the weapons were stored. He then directed the computer to deliver them.

They waited as a robot arm slid under a box, and like a miniature fork lift, raised it off the shelf, then lowered it to the floor.

Michael opened it. It was filled with laser weapons. They were small, almost the size and shape of a square pocket flashlight, and were attached to belts. He handed one to Tara and one to Rebecca. He examined them. "You aim, then press the red button," he said. "I ordered stunners, so these shouldn't kill, they should only knock the guards unconscious." They all put on the belts and placed the weapons in the belts. Then they dragged their supplies out into the corridor.

"The lights are on now," whispered Rebecca. "Why?"

"The guards probably light the corridors as they make their rounds," Michael replied. "Maybe in the excitement of catching

Rachel they forgot to put the lights out. This way," he said, and the girls followed him down the corridor to the door. The supplies were cumbersome. Once they were through the first door, they dragged their boxes to the small blue button on the inner wall and took out their lasers.

"Ready?" asked Michael. They nodded.

Rebecca noticed that her hand with the weapon in it was shaking. Rebecca steadied herself. She had a laser stun gun—no bullets. It was just like the online games she played with her friends. If she shot first no one would die. How hard could it be to outdraw the bad guys?

Michael pressed the blue button. The door opened.

Rachel was seated in a chair directly in front of them. The two guards stood on either side of her. One of them was pointing a small sharp knife at her eye as if he were going to cut her there. Michael shot him and he fell to the floor. Rebecca and Tara both shot at the other, and he, too, fell. All three of them ran to Rachel.

"Rachel, are you all right?" asked Tara, hoarsely.

"She is," came a loud male voice from a darkened corner of the room. "But you aren't. Drop your weapons!" They all turned sideways to see a young guard step into the light and point a laser gun at them.

Rebecca thought she could make out a figure sitting in a chair behind the guard, but there was too little light to really be certain. "Drop those weapons, I said."

Slowly Tara and Rebecca dropped their weapons. Rebecca glanced at Michael. He was still holding his. For a moment

Rebecca thought he wasn't going to drop it, but then she saw his fingers loosen, and the gun clattered to the floor.

The guard moved slowly forward, both hands on his laser, pointing it at Michael, then at Rachel, then at Rebecca, then at Tara, trying to keep them all covered.

"Aeeee!" came a huge scream and someone leaped at the guard's back. The person the guard had been interrogating wrapped his arms around the guard's throat, his legs around the guard's waist. The guard fired his weapon indiscriminately and laser flashes shot erratically around the room. The assailant bent over the guard's neck and bit into it. The guard screamed and dropped his weapon. Michael picked up his stunner and ran over to them.

"It's all right," he said to the boy, who was still clinging to the guard, "you can let him go. Don't move," he ordered the guard. The boy, his red hair falling loosely over his face, slid off the guard, who was clutching his bleeding neck. Michael aimed at the guard and shot. The guard collapsed.

"Jonathan! It's my brother!" Tara ran across the room and hugged him as if she would never let go.

Rebecca could hardly believe her eyes. What was he doing here?

Michael put his hand on Tara's shoulder.

"We've got to go. Now. Your brother can come with us." Jonathon and Tara followed Michael into the hall, but Jonathon had also noticed Rebecca.

"What's *she* doing here?" he asked. "How—?"

"Later." Michael cut him off. "Two of you carry one of

those boxes—I can manage one by myself." He hoisted the large box up into his arms. Rachel and Rebecca grabbed one of the others. Jonathon and Tara grabbed the third. They ran down the corridor until they reached the next door. Instead of pushing the red button leading into the living quarters, however, Michael pressed a small green button on the outer wall. A door slid open. They were facing out into the night.

Michael led the way. The wind was blowing so hard now that the force of it almost knocked them over. Forks of lightning crackled around them and thunder rumbled just above their heads.

Tara screamed. Rebecca was about to snap at Tara to be quiet when she realized that, in the controlled environment of Zanu, Tara would never have seen or heard a storm. At any rate, the scream was stifled by wind and thunder. Rebecca led the way through the forest. The trees were so brittle that the force of the wind was snapping off branches, sending bits and pieces flying into their faces. Rebecca felt a drop of rain on her cheek. Finally, they reached the skimmer and managed to fit all the boxes into its storage compartment. Everyone tumbled in, Michael on the driver's side, Rachel beside him, Rebecca, Tara, and Jonathon in the back.

Michael punched in the co-ordinates, and the small skimmer rose into the air. The wind buffeted it back and forth, tilting it to one side, then another. For a few moments they lurched forward, the pellets of rain pounding the thin surface of the craft.

"I've got to land," shouted Michael above the howl of the

storm. "At least until the wind dies down a bit. Let's just hope we've cleared the water."

He looked at the console. "I think there's a clear spot just below," he shouted. The skimmer tipped from side to side and bobbed up and down. Then with a rude jolt they were on the ground, the storm raging around them.

CHAPTER TWENTY

They sat silently in the skimmer as the storm exploded around them—Michael and Rachel in the front, slumped against the seat in exhaustion; Tara in the back, holding tight to Jonathon's hand; and Rebecca hunched over beside her, biting her nails. And she'd worked so hard to stop biting them—but she didn't care anymore. She couldn't help it—she chewed each one down to the skin, slowly, methodically.

Almost without warning, the storm stopped. The rain became a light drizzle and the wind died down.

"What happened?" asked Tara.

"It seems typical of the weather out here," commented Michael. "Storms blow up out of nowhere and then they're gone. Very erratic." He punched directions into the computer and they lifted off the ground.

"They'll come after us as soon as they can get their air machines off the ground," he said.

"But they'll be looking all around Zanu headquarters, won't they?" asked Rebecca. "They don't know we have a skimmer. They'll think we're trying to escape on foot."

"Yes," agreed Michael, "as long as we can get away fast enough so that they don't see us. Now, if we can just make it back and get the others."

"I hope we're in time for Paul," murmured Tara. She turned to Jonathon. "Are you all right? Did they hurt you?"

"I'm fine," he said, grinning. "They didn't scare me. I'd rather be dead than under their thumb. But what about you, Tara? And Mother and Father?"

Tara looked at Jonathon for a moment, trying to find the right words. There weren't any right words.

"They've taken Mother and Father. Just after that they came for me, but Rebecca and I managed to escape."

"How?" asked Jonathon, bewildered. He looked at Rebecca. "I thought you were safe and sound with *Mark*," he added, a hint of bitterness in his voice.

"I was, but...well..."

"But she was so concerned about me that she tried to help and then we found out that Zanu wants to kill her," Tara finished.

"Why?" asked Jonathon.

"Because their records show that after I disappeared with you, I was never found again," Rebecca answered. "So now they're afraid to let me go back to my time."

Jonathon sat for a moment, absorbing this. When he spoke, his voice was filled with remorse. "Then I ruined everything. If I hadn't gone back to her time, she would have stayed and maybe our time wouldn't be the same."

"Even if that's true," Michael interjected, "we can't say that our time, our present would be better than it is now. Only different. Maybe it was good you brought Rebecca here. Maybe she'll go back and, having seen this future, help change her present so everyone's future is better. We can't know. Look on the bright side!"

As he spoke, he was scanning the monitor for any signs of life. He'd set the coordinates as close as he could to where he thought the rest of their party was located, but spotting the small group of people was much harder than spotting the huge Zanu complex.

"There they are!" He sighed with relief. Rebecca leaned forward. On the small screen were four small blips. Within moments the skimmer was on the ground, its light beams illuminating the little cluster of people.

Michael opened the doors. They all jumped out and ran to the group huddled under the trees. Tara scrambled over everyone to reach Paul. He was lying with his head on Sonya's lap, his face wet with fever.

"Paul," said Tara, "I'm back. And I've got some medicine for you. You're going to be fine now."

Paul stared at Tara, but didn't seem to see her.

"Mommy? You home, Mommy?"

Rachel handed Tara two pills and a water flask. "Can you get him to take them?"

"We've got some medicine for you, Paul. Open your mouth wide," said Tara gently. "You must swallow some medicine."

Paul shook his head and moaned as he twisted from side to side.

Tara licked her forefinger and traced his dry, cracking lips, then slipped her other forefinger and thumb between his lips and placed a pill on his tongue.

"Here, Paul, drink this. Here's some nice, cool water."

Sonya propped up Paul's head and he drank the water and

the pill along with it. Tara slipped another pill into his mouth and held the flask to his lips. Paul gulped and sputtered.

"Carry him to the skimmer," said Michael. "We have to go."

They all crowded into the skimmer. This time it was really a tight squeeze. The skimmer seemed to take longer than usual to lift off, but Rebecca tried to reassure herself that she was imagining this.

"We're very heavy." David's words interrupted her thought. "I hope it can stay afloat."

"We've got to get over the trees, but then what?" Michael said. "Where shall we go?"

There was a temporary silence in the skimmer. Everyone had been so intent on escape that no one had considered where they could establish a camp.

"How should we know?" asked Jonathon, "No one's been here before. One place is as good as the next."

"That's not true," said Rebecca, realizing she had some knowledge to offer. "I've been all over Manitoba."

Even David and Sonya turned their heads partway round to look at Rebecca.

She laughed. "You forget that in my day we travelled wherever we wanted. I've been to lots of places...and I think we should try up north, like around Clear Lake. It's hilly and it'll be cooler there. Maybe we can find some natural shelter. The only problem is, *how* will we find it?"

"Don't worry," answered Michael cheerfully, "just point me in the right direction. I'll find it."

"Well," said Rebecca, trying to remember the map her

father always kept in the glove compartment of their car, "it's northwest of Winnipeg, I think."

"Right!" said Michael, and he set the skimmer's co-ordinates.

The pitch black of the night was beginning to give way to grey, and over the next hour the sun crept above the horizon. No one in the skimmer saw it, though. They were all fast asleep, exhausted from the night's dangers.

When Rebecca did wake up, it was because Paul was twisting and kicking violently and crying, "Mommy, Daddy! Where are you?" She got a sharp kick in the arm before she managed to grasp his legs with both her hands. Jonathon held his arms and Tara stroked his face and tried to soothe him. She gave him more pills and water. Finally he curled up, mostly on Tara, and fell back to sleep.

The sun was climbing in the mid-morning sky. Below them, green forest clung to the hills, which surrounded glistening blue-green lakes.

"It's wonderful," Tara exclaimed. "It's so beautiful."

"It looks almost the same, although I never saw it from the air," said Rebecca. "It doesn't look like it's been harmed at all."

"Let's set down somewhere," Michael suggested.

"There!" Jonathon pointed at a lovely lake near some high hills which sloped gently down to the water.

"Yes," said Rebecca, "I can see some black spots in the hill. They could be caves."

"Once we're out of this skimmer," David cautioned, "their satellites will be able to pick us up. We'll have to find a cave or some covering and stay there until we can work out that problem."

"I think," said Michael, frowning, "that I can disconnect the GPS tracker so that they can't find us but keep it set so that it will still allow us to use it to find our way around."

"Really?" said Rebecca, amazed. "You could do that?"

"I hope so. They were training me to be a programming engineer. I have four years of specialist training. Now, let's see if we can find a big enough cave." He directed the skimmer past a few of the dark openings. One seemed quite large, cut naturally into the face of the hill, about halfway up. Michael let the skimmer hover just in front of it.

"I wonder," he said, "if we can get the whole skimmer in there?"

"Let me check," suggested Jonathon.

"All right," Michael agreed, manoeuvring the craft as close to the opening as he could, and keeping it there, hovering in the air.

The door slid open and Jonathon leapt from the skimmer onto the ledge of the cave. Within moments of disappearing into the black, he was back on the ledge, waving Michael in.

"It's fine!" he shouted. "Deep and lots of room."

Michael turned on the beams and eased the skimmer into the dark cave. The cave seemed to go quite far into the hill, but Michael rested the skimmer close to the edge. He left the beams on and turned on the interior lights. They all got out, except Paul and Tara. Tara didn't want to wake Paul up.

Rebecca looked around. It was a large cave with a high roof. The dirt floor was smooth and level. And, most importantly from Rebecca's viewpoint, there were no bats. In fact, there seemed to be no animals or insects of any kind.

"This will do just fine," Michael said, after looking around. "Our first headquarters. Our first real home," he proclaimed, grinning from ear to ear. "Now, let's break out the food and water and have a celebration!"

Rachel opened the storage compartment of the skimmer and dug around in the boxes until she found a box of food pills. She handed one to each of them and they passed around what was left of their water.

"We can collect more," Michael said, "as soon as I fix this GPS. No one can set foot outside of this cave before I do that. Then we can focus our energies on figuring out how to get Rebecca back to the time machine."

"I'll take her back," said Jonathon.

"What?" Rebecca exclaimed.

"She'll need help. She doesn't know the city, she won't know how to find anything...and I got her here. I'm the one to get her back."

"Jonathon!" cried Tara from the skimmer, trying not to jar Paul as she crawled out from under him and out of the skimmer. "You can't! I can't lose you again. I can't. You're the only family I have left."

A small voice came from the skimmer, "What about me?"

"Paul!" said Tara, turning back to the vehicle.

Paul looked at them all through the door, his eyes clear, his face calm. He frowned at Tara. "I thought I was your brother," he said. "Who's that?" He pointed to Jonathon.

Tara went back to the skimmer, reached in, pulled Paul out

and gave him a huge hug. Then she sat down with him on her lap, her back against the skimmer.

"He's our big brother," she said. "Now you have a sister and a brother."

Paul thought about this for a moment while he looked Jonathon up and down.

"All right," he said. "That's fine, I guess." Then he smiled. "I'm hungry." Tara gave him a big kiss, then took the food pill Rachel handed her and gave it and some water to Paul.

Together, they all sat down by the side of the skimmer, its light penetrating the darkness around them, to plan what seemed impossible: how to get Rebecca back to Winnipeg and safely home.

CHAPTER TWENTY-ONE

Rebecca stood in the beams of the skimmer, holding Tara's hands, trying to find the words to say goodbye. This was no ordinary goodbye. This was forever and they both knew it.

The group had quickly come up with a plan—probably because there were so few options open to them. Michael would take Rebecca and Jonathon to the outskirts of Winnipeg at nightfall. He would let them off at a spot where the force field had to be dissolved every few hours for the incoming high-speed trains which transferred people from city to city. Michael, having worked in all areas of programming, knew where these entered and exited. David and Sonya had told Jonathon to take Rebecca to their home—they knew their children were sympathetic and would help. Once all that had been decided, there was nothing left to do but wait. They sat, talked, and dozed. Jonathon was carefully instructed on the new camp's coordinates. These he was to pass on to the anti-Zanu forces, so they could send people to the camp who were in danger of being cut loose.

Finally, it was time to go.

"I hope you find your parents, Tara," said Rebecca, squeezing Tara' s hand. "And your sister. Try not to worry too much about Jonathon. He'll come back to you. He's so tough nothing will stop him."

Tara looked at Rebecca, her eyes filled with tears. "Be careful," she said, "and get home safely."

Rebecca nodded. She and Tara hugged each other. Rebecca bent and gave Paul a kiss on the head. "No more swimming in the lake," she cautioned him with mock severity.

He laughed. "But maybe the water is nice here. It looks so pretty."

"It just may be," David agreed. "But you'll let us test it first, won't you, Paul?"

Paul drew a circle in the dirt with his toe. "I guess so," he conceded.

Rebecca said goodbye to everyone, then, and climbed into the skimmer.

Tara threw her arms around Jonathon's neck and clung to him. Finally, she loosened her grip and forced herself to back away. She gave him a big smile and said, "See you soon."

Rebecca thought it was the bravest thing she'd seen Tara do. Jonathon climbed into the front seat beside Rebecca and they were off. The blackness surrounded them. For a few short hours they would be relatively safe—but once on the ground, satellites would be able to detect their presence and Zanu guards could track them. They would need a lot of luck to make it safely to David's house. Rebecca thought about home—about Lewis and Catherine, her friends Marta and Lonney. Would she ever get a chance to tell them about this? Probably they were all worried sick. Rebecca hoped for their sake that this time-travel trip would take as little time in her world as the last one had. Assuming she made it back at all!

As if reading her mind, Jonathon said, "Don't worry! Nothing is going to go wrong. You know why? We're a lot smarter than those...those..."

"Goons," Rebecca suggested.

"I don't know what that means," laughed Michael, "but I love the sound of it. Goons. Fits them perfectly."

They flew in silence for the most part, too aware of the danger ahead to feel like talking.

Rebecca found herself thinking about the world she was heading toward, the Zanu world where no one had the right to be different, where no one could choose anything for themselves except what things to buy. Was that happening already in her present? She knew that there were many countries in her world where people had no freedom at all. But somehow, she'd never thought it could happen in Winnipeg. Was everyone so concerned about making money, about their jobs, and about their profits that no one would step up and stop the destruction of their planet and defend their democracy?

Her thoughts were interrupted when a shimmering wall glowed at them through the blackness. It was faint at first but grew stronger and brighter.

Michael flew almost up to the force field, then parallel to it. When he found the right spot, he set the skimmer down.

"We've timed it perfectly," he said. "In a few minutes the train will come along and the force field will be lowered directly ahead of us. I'm going to open the doors now, but you must stay in the skimmer until the force field drops. Then run straight from here into the city. That way the satellites probably won't pick you up."

"What about you?" asked Rebecca. "Can you get out of the way fast enough?"

"Of course!" Michael laughed. "Don't worry about me." He paused. "We'd better say goodbye now." He looked at Rebecca. "I'll miss you. In a way, I wish you could stay and help us."

Rebecca felt herself blushing. "I'll do my best to get back home and help you that way."

Michael looked at Jonathon. "Be careful, Jonathon," he warned. "Don't take any unnecessary chances. Look...it's happening! The force field is dissolving. Get ready."

Rebecca and Jonathon braced themselves. The shimmer in front of them began to evaporate then disappear. A large, clear oval space appeared ahead of them and they could hear the distant hum of the train coming from behind them.

"Go!" yelled Michael.

They pushed themselves out of the skimmer, Jonathon first, then Rebecca. They ran for their lives. The hum of the train was getting louder. Rebecca realized they were running on the track. It wasn't like the train tracks she knew. It was flat and wide and black and hard. Perhaps it was magnetic, she thought, and the train sped along just over its surface. However it travelled, she knew they would soon be caught in the glare of its lights.

"Jump!" Rebecca yelled, and leapt off the track. She landed on her hands and feet, flattened herself to the ground and felt herself rolling downhill. Then Jonathon was tumbling over her and they were in the bottom of a ditch. The train whizzed past, and within a minute, it was gone. Everything was quiet. Rebecca, lying flat on her stomach, raised her head and looked up and around. Jonathon rolled into a crouch.

"Who would ever have thought," Rebecca muttered, "that one day ordinary people, like, not criminals or anything, would be forced to run and hide like scared animals—right here in Winnipeg!"

"They won't! Not if I can help it!" exclaimed Jonathon.

Suddenly they heard the quiet hum of a skimmer. They pressed themselves flat in the bottom of the ditch and held themselves motionless.

The skimmer hummed by. They began to relax. Moments later they heard another hum. It was very close.

"I think Zanu's patrolling the area," Jonathon whispered. "Maybe the train driver reported seeing something. We'll have to keep to the back lanes and move as fast as we can." He crawled up the side of the ditch. "I don't see anything. Let's go!"

Rebecca clambered out of the ditch and they ran toward the nearest back lane. It was difficult trying to run in the dark, never knowing what they could trip over or bump into, but they had no choice. Jonathon led them down the lanes. He counted as they went, to give them a sense of the street numbers. Everything was quiet. No one was out on the streets.

Suddenly he held out his hand. They stopped. A Zanu guard skimmer whizzed by, just as they were coming to a main street. It continued on its way, however, and Rebecca and Jonathon, hearts pounding, ran across the street into another back lane.

"Not far now," said Jonathon. "As we crossed back there I

saw the sign—440 St. North. Six more blocks and we're there."

Rebecca counted as they ran. And then, finally, Jonathon was counting houses. "One, three—here it is," he gasped. "Number five." They ran up to the back window, crouched, and Jonathon knocked gingerly on the window pane. The house was dark—it was well past midnight. No one stirred. He knocked more loudly. Again nothing. "If we ring the door chimes," he whispered, "the computer will record a late-night visitor. Why don't they wake up?" he said, beginning to get frustrated.

Rebecca, every muscle in her body a tense knot, her eyes darting everywhere, was watching for Zanu skimmers. Finally, she could stand it no longer and pounded on the glass with the flat of her hand.

"Ssshhh!" Jonathon grabbed her wrist.

"Well, which is worse? This noise or waiting to get caught by a Zanu patrol?" she hissed.

Suddenly they noticed a pair of eyes staring at them through the glass. Then another pair. Then the eyes disappeared. And within a few moments a young man and a young woman were standing on either side of them. They towered over Rebecca and Jonathon.

"What do you want?" whispered the young woman.

"We were sent here by David and Sonya," Jonathon replied. "They said you'd help us."

"Why should we believe them?" the young man said to the woman. "This could be some kind of trap."

"Look," said Rebecca, "we've risked a lot to get here. They said you'd help us, and we need help."

"Who are you?" asked the young woman.

"I'm Rebecca," she replied. "And this…"

"Wait!" said the woman. "Are you the child from the past?"

"Why, yes," Rebecca replied. "How did you know…?"

"Never mind that," she replied. "Come in, both of you. Follow me straight to my bedroom. We've fixed it so it's safe from that prying computer."

She led the way into the house, through the darkened main room, down the steps, and into her brightly lit room. She was extremely tall, Rebecca saw, as was her brother. Both had long blond hair and green-grey eyes. They were very striking.

"Are you…" Rebecca looked from one to the other. "Are you…"

"Twins. Yes," she replied. "I'm Susan, this is Gary. You're Rebecca, and this is…"

"Jonathon."

"How are my parents?" Susan asked anxiously.

"They're fine," Rebecca answered. "They're hiding up north. We've set up a camp…" Suddenly a wave of dizziness swept over her, there was a buzzing in her ears, and her legs seemed to crumple beneath her. She slumped against the foot of the bed.

"We haven't slept much…and we've been running…" Jonathon explained.

Susan sat down beside Rebecca. "Let's get some blood to your head," she suggested, as she raised Rebecca's knees and gently pressed her head down.

Rebecca found she was panting, her breath coming in erratic gasps.

"Look," said Susan. "You can tell us everything later. How

would you like a hot shower, some fresh clothes, and a great big supper?"

"Yes," Rebecca sighed. "Please."

"Follow me," Susan said to Rebecca and led her to the bathroom. "There's a set of clothes hanging on the hook. Just get into those."

"Thanks," said Rebecca, and she slipped into the bathroom. She took off all her clothes, threw them in a pile, and stepped into the shower stall. Little sprays of soap coated her. Then the water hit her from all sides. She rubbed her hair clean. Then a blast of hot air dried her off. She got dressed. She had to roll the pant legs and the sleeves up about five times, but at least the clothes were clean. They were rather like long black silk pyjamas. She found a brush and did her hair.

By the time she rejoined the others she felt wonderful but still a little lightheaded from hunger.

Jonathon then took his turn and Rebecca plunked herself down on the bed. Susan had put a tray on a small, round, clear plastic table. She pushed the table right up to the bed.

"You'd better eat something," she advised. Rebecca dug into what looked like a real piece of meat, and real vegetables, but which tasted tart.

"Kelp," said Gary.

She was drinking a glass of clear, cold water when Jonathon came into the bedroom, clean and dressed in some of Gary's clothes—also with pants and sleeves rolled up. He ate, then they both sank against the bed, on the thick grey carpet, ready to answer questions.

"Your parents are fine," said Rebecca. "Better than could be expected, really."

"What do you mean by that?" asked Gary.

"Just that if we hadn't escaped they'd probably be dead soon—now at least they have a chance." Rebecca recounted how she had come to their world, her meeting with David and Sonya, and all the events right up until she and Jonathon had knocked on their window.

"And you," Gary said to Jonathon when Rebecca had finished, "are hoping we'll help you set up some kind of underground resistance."

"Yes," said Jonathon gravely.

"Pretty dangerous work, don't you think?"

"Yes."

The twins grinned at each other, then beamed at Jonathon and Rebecca.

Susan laughed aloud and explained, "We've already begun! You've come to the right place. We already have a system of bypassing the Zanu frequencies and we're coordinating all the anti-Zanu forces from a safe house. We've set up a network of safe houses all over the city, so that people who suspect they're about to be cut loose can go underground instead. Now that you have a camp established up north, people will have a second option—they can make their way up there by sneaking out of the city the same way you snuck in."

Jonathon was stunned.

"I can't believe it! Why, you're doing exactly what I had planned..."

"There are more people than you realize, Jonathon," said Gary, "who feel the same way we do. And now that we know that the disintegrator isn't just used for objects, I think more and more will join us."

"Can I stay here?" Jonathon asked.

"Not here," Susan replied. "I'm afraid you'd be terribly restricted. And it's not right for a young boy like you to be stuck in one room, day after day!"

"It doesn't matter," replied Jonathon. "At least I'm free here, I'm not being re-educated or disintegrated, and I can do something to help. Tara will understand if I don't go back right away. I'll get her a message somehow."

"So it's our job to get Rebecca back to her time. But when?" Susan mused. "And how? It won't be easy. The first thing we have to do is to find out about the security on the time machine, and then plan a strategy with our people. We'll do that in the morning. But now you'll have to be moved."

"What!" exclaimed Rebecca and Jonathon together.

"Yes, you'll have to be moved," repeated Susan. "This house is not safe. Because of our parents, we're very high risk. We're watched constantly. While you were cleaning up, I contacted someone—they're going to pick you up and take you to the safe house."

Just then they heard a faint scratching against the wall.

"He's here," Gary said.

"Right," said Susan. "We may not see you again. You'll be safe where you're going. Do exactly as you're told and we'll all hope for the best. You'll have to travel in the storage compartment.

Just run out to the skimmer, jump in, and the top will be fastened down." She held out her hand to each of them.

"Good luck," she said as they shook hands.

"Good luck," Gary echoed as he, too, held out his hand. "Follow me," he said.

He led them out of Susan's bedroom, up the steps and through the darkened central area to the front door, which slid open. They could just make out the skimmer waiting for them in the street. They ran to it, then hopped into the storage area in the back. Rebecca tried to see their escort but it was too dark. Someone closed the compartment and they were moving.

It seemed like hours, but Rebecca knew it was probably no more than ten minutes later when the door was opened and a young man's voice whispered, "Here we are. Run to the house. I'll close up after you."

They leaped out and ran from the back to the front of the house. Their escort put his hand on a milky square; it glowed red, the door opened. They hurried inside.

"Follow me," the voice said.

That's strange, Rebecca thought. That voice...I swear I've heard it before.

He led them into the central area, then pushed the button on the floor. The floor panel slid back. He guided them down the unlit stairs, then pushed the wall button opening a door on the left. Once in the room, he shut the door and turned on the light.

"Mark!" both Rebecca and Jonathon exclaimed at the same time.

He smiled. "I thought I'd never see either of you again."

"But…but…" Jonathon was quite speechless.

"I've been working against Zanu since my eleventh birthday, Jonathon," Mark said, plopping himself onto the bed.

"But…then why…why did you…"

"Why did I go after you? Well, I didn't have much time to think it over—I just felt that you might start things which we couldn't control. At least we were developing ways to fight here—you could have made things better—or much worse."

"And I did make them worse—I somehow did just what history says I did—managed to spirit Rebecca away…" said Jonathon. "Maybe the future's all set," he added, "and we're just doing what we have to do…"

"Maybe," Mark said. "But if we can get Rebecca back, then we know that's not so."

"But…" said Jonathon, "I always thought you were all *for* Zanu…"

"I couldn't tell you, Jonathon," said Mark. "You were too unpredictable. We were afraid you'd do something rash, get us and yourself into trouble."

For a moment the two friends just looked at each other. Rebecca thought she understood what was going on. They had been best friends, had lost each other, then found they were even closer than they thought. Mark got off the bed and went up to Jonathon. Soon they were hugging, laughing, and hugging again. Rebecca beamed at them both.

"You certainly fooled me," she said to Mark.

"I had to," he tossed back. "It's my cover."

"Then...it was you who tipped people off—who helped Tara and me escape."

Mark nodded. "Tell me what happened," he said.

They sat on the bed and Rebecca told him what had happened to her and Tara since leaving in the middle of the night. He listened with great interest. As she drew near the end of the story, Jonathon began to tell Mark what had happened to him after he had been cut loose. Rebecca crawled under the covers of the bed. Mark and Jonathon's voices began to drift to her from farther and farther away. It was three a.m. and she hadn't slept for...how long? She was too tired to figure it out. The bed was so wonderful, the sheets were silky and cool, the comforter light but warm. Idly, she wondered if it was a waterbed—or maybe it was made of air?

That was her last thought before she fell into a deep, much needed sleep.

CHAPTER TWENTY-TWO

Rebecca opened her eyes. She was lying in a strange bed in a strange room, and for a moment she really couldn't remember where she was. Somehow, though, she knew she was glad to be in a real bed and to be smelling real food…Oh! She sat up. Mark was entering the room, a tray in his hand. He set it down on a small, round, clear plastic table beside the bed. He smiled.

"Good morning. Did you sleep well?"

"I…I…guess I did," Rebecca replied. She looked at the food and the drink, steam rising from the cup. "What is it?" she asked.

"Toasted kelp bread, fruit, and iced tea," Mark said with a grin.

"Oh…" Rebecca tried to look enthusiastic. "Real iced tea?"

"Real iced tea, and very rare, I might add. I thought you might enjoy it." He sat down on the edge of the bed.

The toast was edible, if tart, the fruit tasted slightly bitter, and the tea was great. All in all, after her experience up north, it was a wonderful breakfast.

"Where's Jonathon?" she asked, as she drank the last of her iced tea.

"Just finishing breakfast in my room," Mark said. "I've told him to come in here when he's dressed and ready—it's almost eleven a.m. and our people have been very busy planning your escape. Everything is arranged."

"Already?"

"Yes. The longer you're in Zanu, the greater the chances are you'll be caught. I've already been out and bought clothes for you and Jonathon. Naturally Jonathon will have to stay here, in hiding, for the moment. You will be picked up by Kevin at 11:30. He'll drive you to the museum, where the time machine is kept. It's under very heavy guard since Jonathon and I used it, but we've planned a diversion and we'll be armed. Kevin has the coordinates he'll need to program the time machine so it will get you home. As a backup, at least five other people also have the information, should things get rough. Your job is to get yourself into that machine. And home. Somehow, then, history as we know it will change..." He paused. "What, I wonder, will that mean?"

Rebecca looked at him thoughtfully. "Do you think you could all be—sorry about this, but—*wiped out* in that one second when I get home?"

She hoped he would laugh, tell her that she was being over imaginative. But he didn't.

"It's possible," he said.

"But then why are you so anxious to send me back? I could stay, and we could change things here. I don't want to be responsible for wiping out billions of people!"

Now he did smile, a little.

"I only said possible. After all, how would I know? Probably we'll all be here—but maybe something you do in your future will change our present...or maybe just changing our history will cause all sorts of different possibilities."

"Different ribs on the fan…" Rebecca mused.

"Yes, exactly," agreed Mark. "We all feel it's a chance we'll have to take." Again he paused for a moment. "The only thing that really bothers me," he said finally, "is that if things do change radically the second you get back to your world—we probably won't know the difference. All of a sudden we'll be the same people but with different histories and we won't remember any of this."

"You won't remember me," Rebecca said softly.

"True," Mark admitted.

"And," Rebecca was getting agitated, "I'll never know what happened to everyone here…"

"Of course, there is one other possibility," Mark interrupted.

"What?"

"Nothing will change. Except there might be an additional rib somewhere, another universe added with a changed future and that one will be different."

"But even if my going back doesn't change things, *you'll* change things," Rebecca said with a smile. "I know you will. Now that you have a base up north and people here working…"

"Well," said Mark. "Nothing will happen if we sit here all day. I've got to get you ready. They'll be here for you any minute! Your clothes are hanging in the bathroom."

When Rebecca returned to the bedroom, washed and dressed in her new clothes—shocking-pink silk pants and top, with gold boots—Jonathon and Mark were waiting for her.

"Kevin is outside," said Mark. "Just walk out to the skimmer and get in. Act as naturally as you can. I'll disable the computer for about fifteen seconds, short enough to not register, long enough for you to get out of here."

Rebecca looked at them both and hesitated. She had been desperate to get home ever since she arrived, but suddenly everything seemed to be happening too fast.

"You have to go *now*," said Mark. Rebecca knew he was right. Impulsively, she kissed Mark and Jonathon each on the cheek, then, without a word, left the bedroom, walked with them up the stairs, waited until Mark gave her a nod and then let herself out.

A small red skimmer hovered just above the road, right in front of the house.

She forced herself to walk calmly down the sidewalk and get into the skimmer.

"Hello," said a small young man with curly dark hair and dark eyes. "Ready?"

She nodded and attempted a smile.

They drove down the street toward the centre of town. They were just entering the busy section of the city when a Zanu guard skimmer pulled up beside them and motioned them to stop.

"Keep calm," said Kevin under his breath, as two Zanu guards approached their windows, one on either side.

Kevin pushed the controls and the windows rolled down.

"Routine I.D. check," said the guards.

Rebecca's turned cold with fear. She sat, hands in her lap, and tried to look calm. Any show of fear would make them suspicious.

"Certainly," Kevin said, smiling. He reached for a small

compartment on the front of the skimmer. As he did so, Rebecca saw his hand stray to the computer. Suddenly the skimmer rocketed forward and away from the guards. Rebecca looked behind her. The guards were drawing their weapons, but Kevin already had the skimmer turning a corner and racing down a side street. They were entering into the busy part of town at a tremendous speed, passing other skimmers, almost running people down as they moved over sidewalks when necessary.

Then, on a very busy shopping street, Kevin said, "We've got to dump the skimmer and walk now. Get out. We'll lose ourselves in the crowd."

They both got out of the skimmer and waded into the sea of people. Kevin grasped Rebecca's hand tightly.

"Not too fast," he continued. "We don't want to draw any attention to ourselves."

He pulled her through the jostling crowds until finally they were climbing the museum steps. They walked through the small exhibit rooms and into the huge display room which housed the time machine. It reminded Rebecca of an igloo. It even had a long, curved, igloo-like entrance leading into it. Along the walls of the huge room were displays of various kinds of housing—tents, caves, grass huts, miniature brick buildings, log cabins. Teachers and their students were milling around them.

Rebecca stayed as close to Kevin as she could, watching his every move. She saw him nod, but couldn't see who he was nodding to. Someone must have seen the signal, though, because suddenly the grass hut and log cabin were in flames, and people were screaming and running in all directions. Some of the guards left their posts around the time machine, but most stood their ground and jerked to attention, lasers ready. In the next moment, however, they all crumpled to the floor. Amidst the panic, the anti-Zanu people had each taken out one guard with their stun guns.

Kevin pulled Rebecca forward. Rebecca saw laser flashes all around them. More guards were converging on the room and the anti-Zanu forces were fighting them off.

Kevin and Rebecca ducked into the long, white tunnel. A huge computer console was built into one of the walls. They ran alongside it toward a door at the far end of the tunnel. Kevin pressed a button on the wall and the door slid up.

"Get in!" Kevin ordered. "Quick!"

"But what about you?" asked Rebecca.

"Never mind! We have an escape plan. Now go!" Kevin commanded, his finger on the button for the door.

Rebecca stepped back into the central compartment of the time machine. Kevin pushed the button, then dashed to the computer console. The white door slid down, then everything was deathly quiet.

She was having that strange sensation again: the sensation of the world going soft.

PART THREE

CHAPTER TWENTY-THREE

Rebecca was standing by the duck pond. A child of about six was pointing at her and screaming. The child's mom was saying, "That's just your imagination, Sam!" The mom threw an apologetic look at Rebecca and said, "He thinks you're an alien."

A wave of dizziness passed over Rebecca and she staggered slightly.

"Are you all right?" the woman asked.

"Yes, yes, fine," said Rebecca.

Rebecca gazed up at the sky and saw that the sun was well on its way to setting. Well, it was at least a half-hour walk from the park to her house so Rebecca figured she'd better get moving.

She smiled at the young boy, who clutched his mother even tighter, waved, and set off at a slow jog.

Soft, warm air caressed her skin. She could smell freshly cut grass and flowers. She breathed deeply. She glanced at the familiar houses, the quiet tree-lined streets, the kids playing outside. Even little children were still up, their parents watching them from the front steps. It was too warm and beautiful for anyone to be inside.

Oh, I'm glad to be back! Rebecca thought.

By the time she reached Cordova, she was tired and out of breath. She turned onto the sidewalk to her house and saw that the door was open, the screen door closed. She managed the three steps to the landing, tried the inner door, but found it was locked. She rang the bell and smoothed down her top.

Oh no! How was she going to explain these clothes? The explanation was not going to be easy. And what was the date? Was she about to return to a house frantic about her disappearance or had she once again been lucky and sent back only hours later? Well, it was evening and she had left in the afternoon so they were bound to be pretty worried at the very least.

Rebecca stared at the white stucco surrounding the green door and waited impatiently. Green? But that wasn't possible. They had painted it mustard last week. She'd helped with the painting the day before the picnic. Why had they changed it back to green? Of course, mustard was the one colour in the world she hated. But after all that work, why would they repaint it? Finally her mother opened the door.

"Hi, Mom! I'm home!" Rebecca exclaimed.

"Rebecca? I thought you were in your room reading." She paused. "And where did you get those clothes?"

Uh oh, thought Rebecca.

"You haven't missed me?" she asked tentatively.

"You know I love you, sweetheart, but I saw you five minutes ago."

Rebecca wasn't sure what to say. So she asked the first thing that came to mind. "Why did you repaint the front of the house? I mean, I hated that mustard, but I thought you liked it."

"We're painting the house Friday, Rebecca," said her mom. "What's going on?"

"Oh hi, Rebecca," said Lewis, as he ran down the stairs to the main hallway. "I thought you were reading. Hey, where'd you get those clothes?"

"Rebecca," remarked Catherine, coming into the hallway from the kitchen, "have you decided about going to the demonstration yet?"

Rebecca looked at Catherine, at Lewis, and at her mother. She felt a growing sense of panic. "I need some air," she muttered. Somehow she managed to reach the front door and collapse on the steps outside. She gulped the cool night air. She felt the cold steps through her thin clothes. She put her hands flat on either side of her, feeling the concrete. That, at least, was real. She tried to slow her breathing. She knew there was an explanation and she suspected she knew just what it was. But that would mean....

When Kevin set the time machine, in all that chaos, he did it wrong. He had sent her back—early. But how early?

Rebecca could hear her mother calling her.

"Honey, come in, please. Are you okay?"

"Really, Mom, I'm fine," she yelled back.

"Mom! Mom! Can you come up here, please?"

Rebecca sat on the step, her heart pounding. Who had just called from her room? It had sounded unmistakably like herself.

"I thought you were outside," Rebecca heard her mom call up the stairs. Then the phone rang and her mom hurried into the kitchen to answer it.

At that moment both Lewis and Catherine walked up to the screen door.

"Hey!" said Lewis. "What is this? I just heard you call from upstairs."

Rebecca closed her eyes. She had to think.

"Mom!" the voice came again. "I have to ask you something."

"Rebecca," said Lewis, "what are you up to?"

Catherine came out, tucked her long legs beneath her, and sat on the steps beside Rebecca. She pulled her thick hair out of her eyes, and stared at her new sister.

"You're acting very strangely," she said. "What's going on?"

Rebecca felt paralyzed. What should she say? What should she do? She swatted at a mosquito that was buzzing around her ear.

"Let's go into the sunroom and talk," said Lewis. Lewis hated mosquitoes.

Rebecca got up and motioned them ahead of her to the sunroom.

She sank into a striped lawn chair. Lewis and Catherine sat down, too. They didn't bother to turn on the light because light from the dining room filtered through the screen door.

"That is some outfit," declared Catherine.

"Yeah," Rebecca sighed, "beautiful, isn't it? But you're not going to believe where I got it."

She took a deep breath, then plunged right in.

"I've been to another future. A totally different one."

"That's not possible," said Lewis with great authority. "*We* come from the future. What do you mean, *another* one?"

"I mean," said Rebecca firmly, "that I was in the park, on this picnic on Saturday—"

"Wait," interrupted Lewis, holding up his hand, "the picnic isn't until this coming Saturday. We haven't been to a picnic yet."

"What day is it?" Rebecca asked.

"Wednesday," Lewis and Catherine said together.

For a moment Rebecca paused, trying to take that in. And then she continued. She recounted the strange future world she'd just experienced—a future totally different from the one that Lewis and Catherine knew so well. When she reached the end, she paused to gauge their reactions.

For a moment Lewis and Catherine just sat and looked at her. Then they looked at each other. It seemed to Rebecca that they could communicate without exchanging words. Rebecca could practically hear them thinking, going over the possibilities, wondering how her story could even be possible.

They both turned back to her at the same moment.

"We believe you," Catherine said. "But do you realize what this means?"

"Mom!" Someone was running down the stairs. Through the screen on the sunroom door Rebecca, Lewis, and Catherine had a clear view of the kitchen.

Rebecca's mother was hanging up the phone.

"Mom! I've been calling you. I need help understanding this section of the book I'm reading. It's a little too deep for me!"

Someone was standing beside her mother in the kitchen, showing her the book.

Lewis and Catherine looked at the kitchen, then looked at Rebecca. Rebecca couldn't take her eyes off the girl in the kitchen.

"Yes, I realize what it means," Rebecca said, her voice a dry whisper. "I would still be here, up in my room, reading and researching nuclear energy—which is what I remember doing all last Wednesday night."

CHAPTER TWENTY-FOUR

It was a huge shopping mall. The size of four square city blocks. It had water fountains surrounded by palm trees and weeping willows. White orchids grew next to purple crocuses in long flower beds along the main concourse and every few yards there were bright red geraniums in cedar pots. Mannequins were modelling silks and satins, and little robots were speeding around helping the shoppers. Jonathon felt exhilarated. What should he buy first? Perhaps that beautiful painting, a portrait of a city made out of triangular red shapes. He stopped a robot and gave it his card. The robot took the card in its slim metal hand and popped it into its mouth. The robot's eyes lit up red. A nasty beeping howl emanated from its head. Suddenly Jonathon was surrounded by guards.

"You didn't buy your quota for last week!" one guard shouted.

"You'll have to come with us," commanded another.

Jonathon was terrified. But there was a young girl with short brown hair peering out from behind a palm tree, signalling to him. He had the feeling she was going to help him. Then he felt the gun stick into his back. "Move!"

Jonathon sat bolt upright in bed. He was drenched in sweat. His hair felt clammy on his neck. He looked around, sighed, and flopped back onto his pillow. A dream. It had all been a dream.

He forced himself up again. He felt disoriented. What day was it? What time was it? He looked at the wall beside his bed. A slim rectangle had been cut into the pale red. He passed his hand over it. Wednesday, July 6, 40 N.E. 8:02 a.m. He passed his hand over it again and the writing disappeared. He had a space training class in an hour, but somehow he didn't feel like going. He flopped back down on his air bed. It was soft and, as always, the perfect temperature.

Maybe he'd just lie in bed today and read. But read what? No, he was already in trouble. Why did he want to read books that no one else was interested in? Why did he have to be *different*?

And that dream. It was the third time this week he'd had a dream like that. That girl was becoming so familiar to him that he felt he knew her. Who was she, and why did he keep dreaming about her? And why did he keep having these nightmares about a world where there were police and guns, and where you were forced to buy things?

Of course he knew what police were. He'd read about them. But there hadn't been police in his lifetime. Or in his mother's. His grandmother's, yes. And his great-grandmother's, definitely. They'd told him stories about police. But this strange idea of being punished for not *buying*? He'd never heard of that. No. That must be all in his imagination.

Suddenly, Jonathon felt restless. He leapt out of bed, and headed for the bathroom.

After a hot shower, he put on a pair of blue cotton shorts and a blue short-sleeved top. He surveyed his room. What a mess. His bed stood against the straight inner wall. Between that and the curved outer wall, there was a desk and an air chair, but you could barely see them because they were covered in books, as was the gleaming wood floor. He made himself a promise. This afternoon, I'll at least clear off my desk. I really must do some space work this afternoon.

His house, like all Winnipeg houses, was built on a circular plan. The eating area was in the centre, along with a family room and a computer room. This central area was surrounded by bedrooms. Solar-powered skylight panels let light in through the ceiling; coverings could be drawn over them in the sleeping quarters.

Jonathon sat down in the kitchen area. The house was quiet. His parents must have left already, and Tara was apprenticing in the aqua station at the zoo, connected virtually to the real aqua station in Vancouver. He'd eat later. He grabbed a bun that the stove had just baked and ran out the back door into the small courtyard, which was dominated by a large apple tree. The snapdragons and geraniums around the apple tree only left room for a small patch of lawn and a smooth concrete surface for skimmers. Jonathon got into his skimmer and manoeuvred it into the air above the houses. He had to go see his great-grandmother. She was the only one who seemed to understand him. He had to talk to someone about these dreams.

It was a beautiful day. The sky was a deep blue, with cumulus clouds blowing in from the west. The city flowed white beneath him. All the buildings were connected, the downtown offices branching out to connect with the residential houses. They were all round, except where they connected, and there they dipped slightly, giving the impression of gentle snowdrifts. Of course, in winter they were all tinted a pale red, which looked warm and inviting against the pure white snow. Ground vehicles had long since been scrapped and now everyone either walked or, for long distances, used their skimmers. In the winter, if you didn't mind the walk, you could cross the entire city without ever going outside, since each house or building had an enclosed walkway built along its outer wall.

Within minutes Jonathon was at his great-grandmother's home. He landed his skimmer and walked to the back door. He passed his hand over a small red beam located in the centre of the door and the door slid up.

"Hello!" he called as he stepped into the house.

"Hello!" he heard a voice call from her bedroom.

"Coming!"

Her bedroom door slid open and she walked over to Jonathon with slow deliberate steps. He kissed her on the cheek. She was a small woman, her face lined and creased, her white hair cut short. But she walked with a straight back, her brown eyes were bright, and she never complained that her back often hurt and she tired too easily.

They sat on the couch.

"I had that dream again," Jonathon said morosely. "Why do I keep having that stupid dream?"

She smiled at him and patted his hand. "Maybe it's trying to tell you something."

"It? What?" Jonathon said. "After all, *it* is *me*. I'm creating that dream."

"Some things," his great-grandmother said carefully, "are not explained so easily. Did you know," she continued after a pause, "that there is a museum in the city?"

"What's a museum?" Jonathon asked, a little nervously. This sounded like one of his great-grandmother's odd, *individual* ideas. After all, she was the one who had suggested that he read *The Lord of the Rings,* and all of Hans Christian Andersen, and all of Mark Twain. And then he'd found he was the only one reading those books.

Not that anyone cared what he read. He was free to do as he pleased, but he didn't like feeling different all the time, doing different things than everyone else.

But he liked the books. A lot. Was this 'museum' going to make him feel the same way? Both good and bad?

"A museum," she replied with a laugh, "is a place where you can find out about the past."

"Who cares about the past?" Jonathon answered, feeling grumpy. "Everything's great now. The past was just a mess. I mean, I love the stories in those books I'm reading, but at the same time I hate reading them. They're full of poverty and violence and..."

"I just thought," his great-grandmother carried on, "that you might find it interesting. It's near the city centre; your skimmer computer will direct you there. It's called the The Museum of Man."

Jonathon sighed.

"Are you going to tell me *why* you think I might find it interesting?"

She looked at him very seriously.

"I know this is hard for you, Jonathon. But you'll find the answers if you keep looking."

Jonathon managed a weak smile in return. Why did his great-grandmother always have to sound so mysterious? She was the only one who seemed to understand him, and yet he could never get a straight answer out of her.

"All right," he agreed, getting up, "I'll go see this museum of yours. Maybe it has something in it about dreams."

"Maybe it does," she smiled.

Jonathon programmed his skimmer for The Museum of Man, and in ten minutes he was in an almost empty skimmer lot large enough for at least thirty skimmers. He walked to the outer door, which slid up as he approached. As he entered, an elderly man, probably in his nineties, looked up from an air chair near the door. He beamed at Jonathon.

"Ah," he exclaimed, "a visitor! A visitor! How nice, how nice! Do come in. Would you like a tour? The full tour?"

"Yes, please. That would be, um, great," Jonathon answered, feeling sorry for the old man. Obviously, he didn't get to give the "full tour" all that often.

Jonathon was shown everything: costume displays, vehicle displays, mechanical displays, and artefacts. It was all slightly dusty, as if no one really cared about any of it anymore. There was even a huge golden statue standing alone in one room, covered in dust. Finally, at the end of the tour, he was taken through the housing display.

He saw thatched cottages, mud huts, small replicas of brick buildings and skyscrapers, and, in the centre, a white igloo. Actually he found it all surprisingly interesting—and yet, here was that awful feeling again. Why should he find history interesting when everyone else found it completely irrelevant and useless?

"Of course," said his guide, "the First Nations people lived in these up north. But this isn't just an igloo, oh no," he said, pointing at the white structure covered in grey dust. "No, this is also our time machine!"

"What!" Jonathon exclaimed.

"Yes, it's not used anymore. We had a number of unfortunate "incidents" and since then no one's felt it was very wise to use it."

Jonathon stared at the white igloo. A long curved entrance protruded out the front. It looked familiar— but where had he seen it before? He felt drawn to it—fascinated by it. What would it be like to travel through time?

What was he thinking? No one used it because the past was horrible. No one was interested. So why was he? What was the matter with him? And why did great-grandmother's help always turn out to be so confusing? He stared at the time machine. No, he'd have nothing to do with it. Nothing. He thanked the guide and quickly left the building.

As he reached his skimmer he stopped short. He'd just remembered where he'd seen the time machine. Not in an old book, or an old tape. He'd seen it in his dreams. And suddenly, he didn't know why, but he knew that somehow, he just had to use it.

CHAPTER
TWENTY-FIVE

Rebecca suddenly felt limp and dizzy. Catherine, practical as always, took over. "Rebecca, you look terribly pale. I'm going to get you something to drink. Have you eaten?"

Rebecca realized she hadn't eaten since Mark had given her kelp for breakfast. She shook her head.

Catherine got up and went into the kitchen.

Rebecca and Lewis sat in silence until Catherine returned with a tray, food and three glasses of juice. Rebecca gulped her orange juice down, then quickly ate most of the cheddar and bread on the plate. She bit into a peach and sighed with pleasure.

"Oh, thank you! That's better. No wonder I was feeling so dizzy." Although she knew the reason wasn't just physical.

"Logically, of course," said Lewis, sipping his juice, "this makes perfect sense. Today is Wednesday. You haven't left for the future yet. That doesn't happen until the picnic on Saturday. They sent you back half a week early. So here you are. And," he pointed to the kitchen, "*there* you are."

"But it can't be," cried Rebecca. "How can there be two of me? Who's the real me? How do I get back to being one again?" She paused. "Should we tell Mom? She'll probably think she's losing her mind if we don't tell her something. How can I be two places at once?"

"I don't know," said Catherine slowly, "she's had a lot to deal with—just accepting *our* story."

"There's something else," Lewis interrupted. "How much do we dare to change things in these next three days? If we tell your mom, there's one more person who knows and perhaps the fewer the better."

"Why?" asked Rebecca.

"I'm not sure," answered Lewis, "only think about this: do you remember everything you did from now until the Saturday picnic?"

"Well," answered Rebecca, taking her time to think back, "not every little detail, but a fair amount, though of course we wouldn't have had that *exact* same talk on the Wednesday that I was here. We only talked about the book I was reading on nuclear energy, not about going into a different future."

Lewis pondered. "Things are already changing then," he stated. "Unless," he stopped for a moment, then held his head in his hands as if to keep the thought inside, "unless this is the way it has always happened."

Rebecca thought back to a week ago. "I'm not sure. Some things seem very clear. Others seem like big fuzzy blanks."

"I think," Lewis said, "we should be very careful about changing things. The future might change and Jonathon might not come back here."

"Or maybe we *should* change it," Catherine suggested. "After all, why should Rebecca have to go through all that danger again?"

"Because," Lewis replied, "I can only see one way for her to become a whole person again. That is to go into the future.

Maybe that moment on Saturday when she is supposed to go into the future is the moment in which she will become one again. Rebecca, when you were in the future was there one of you or two?"

"One," replied Rebecca. "At least, as far as I know."

"Let's assume then that there was just one," said Lewis. "In that case, we have to get you into the future if you ever want to be *only* one again."

Rebecca got to her feet and began to pace back and forth.

"*If* I want to be one again?" she muttered. "Boy, do I ever! I can't stay as two people. Good grief, what would Mom do with two of me? What would *I* do with two of me? There's not even room for her in my room."

"That's true," Catherine laughed. "I mean, there's not enough space for one of you in that mess, never mind two."

Rebecca glared at her. Catherine wouldn't make a mess anywhere. She was too perfect. But Rebecca was more concerned about other things.

What would happen with my friends? she thought. Every time I wanted to call Marta on the phone, she'd be talking to *her*. I'd have to share my clothes. My books. What if—what if my friends liked the other me better? No, that couldn't be. After all, they were the same.

Aloud she said, "If I have to go back to Zanu on Saturday to get back to being one, then I'll do it. But do I have to relive all that danger—being cut loose, chased, almost killed?"

"I don't see any other way," Lewis said.

"Wait a minute," said Catherine, "why were they so afraid

to send you back here, Rebecca? The rulers of Zanu, I mean, not your friends."

"Well," explained Rebecca, "they were afraid I'd change things in some way and that, as a result, big business wouldn't grow so powerful and they might not even exist. They said that once I disappeared, I never came back here, so just sending me back would probably change things."

"That's it!" exclaimed Catherine. "That's it!"

Rebecca looked at Catherine in confusion.

"What's it?"

"Well, just you being here right now changes things. And what if you can also change something else, do something different—I mean, if we can get the other Rebecca to change something over the next few days, I'll bet the future you go into won't be the same. Maybe it won't be dangerous."

"But then why would Jonathon want to escape from it?" Rebecca countered. "If I or she, or we, oh, I don't know, if *Rebecca*, changes it," she said finally, referring to herself in the third person, "Jonathon might not appear. And then I've missed my chance to become one again."

"I suppose," Lewis said, "it would be possible for Jonathon to come back anyway."

"It's very risky," said Rebecca, "because if Jonathon doesn't come back, I'll never get to go into the future and become one person again!"

"Even if he does," said Lewis, "you could become one again but then be killed in the future. Sounds like you were lucky last time. Your luck might not hold this time."

"It was a corporate society, you said." Catherine was thinking out loud. "One big business. What could happen? What could you do differently over the next few days that you didn't do last time?"

Rebecca thought. She started going over everything out loud. "I worked, you bugged me about that demonstration a lot, we painted the house—"

"Just a minute," Catherine interrupted. "You didn't go to the demonstration with me, did you?"

"No," said Rebecca, "I was too busy."

"Well," suggested Catherine, "that's a possibility. I want to stage a demonstration outside a factory in St. Boniface. This big multinational corporation runs it and the factory is polluting the air and the water supply. If you came, *that* would be doing something different. You could get your friends to come and it would be a larger, more forceful group."

"Yes," Lewis stated decidedly. "That's it. Catherine, you and I have to get Rebecca to go to that demonstration."

"You don't have to convince me," said Rebecca, "I'll do it."

"No, no," said Lewis, "it can't be you. You have to stay out of sight. It has to be the original Rebecca."

"But why can't I go? After being to Zanu and seeing that world wrecked by pollution from big corporations, I know how important something like this is."

"That's just it," answered Lewis. "You know too much, you'd be interfering with time. It has to be a free choice by the Rebecca in this time line."

"Well, let me tell me," exclaimed Rebecca. "I'd believe myself!"

"No," said Lewis firmly, "somehow I don't think the two of you should meet until Saturday."

"Why not?" demanded Rebecca.

"Look," Lewis replied, "we need Jonathon to come to our time, right?"

"Right," replied Catherine and Rebecca.

"But we need to change things so that when Rebecca goes to the future with him, she can first of all become one again and secondly find herself in a better future where she is no longer in danger. Right?"

"Right," they replied.

"So," he continued, "we need a small change. A positive change. Like the demonstration. But what if the two Rebeccas met? We have no idea what could happen then. Once you meet each other, the change is gigantic. Two Rebeccas interacting with each other? Who knows how that could change our future! Maybe we'd all suddenly turn into doubles. Or maybe we'd all be blotted out, or maybe we'd create an even worse future."

"A lot of maybes," Rebecca retorted.

"Then, of course," Catherine added, "there is the grandfather paradox of time. We studied it when we worked on our time machine."

"The what?" Rebecca said.

"The grandfather paradox," Lewis said. "Imagine that you go into the past and meet your grandfather. And you kill him. Then you'd never be born, so how could you kill him? Don't you see? It's too dangerous to meet yourself—we just don't know what will happen."

"Well, Lewis," Rebecca said slowly, "you may be right. But maybe I'm right. The other me has gone back upstairs. I'm going to try to meet myself."

And with that she rose from her chair and walked through the dining room to the hallway stairs, Lewis and Catherine following behind her. But as she climbed, each step seemed a huge effort. She reached the upstairs hallway, her legs feeling heavy and wooden. The door to her room was only a few steps away. She lifted her hand to turn the knob. Her arm felt as if it was made of lead. The knob seemed to go soft under her touch and everything around her felt like it was melting. A wave of dizziness passed through her. She thought she was going to be sick. She couldn't move. Lewis and Catherine turned her from the door and guided her back down the stairs and into the sunroom, and sat her in a lawn chair.

"How are you?" Lewis asked, like a doctor speaking to a patient.

"Actually," Rebecca answered, surprised, "not that bad—now." She'd felt so terrible just a few moments before.

"Well," Lewis declared, "I guess that settles that."

"That settles what?" Rebecca asked.

"You can't meet yourself. That's why you became sick. It is physically impossible."

"Okay," she sighed. She certainly didn't want a repeat of that experience. "You win. I'll go into hiding. But where?"

"I think you'll be all right in my room," Catherine suggested. "As long as you aren't in the same room with her. You may not feel great being that close, but I don't think we have much choice. We'll have to be very careful."

"That's the understatement of the year," said Rebecca.

"You two wait here," suggested Catherine. "I'll go see if I can convince Rebecca to go to this meeting Friday morning."

"'Wait a minute," Rebecca said. "Maybe I can help. After all, who knows me better than me? Let's see, what would make me want to go?"

She thought for a moment. Well, if Cath is asking, I'm probably saying no just to show her I don't have to do everything she tells me. I hate feeling pushed around by Lewis and Cath. On the other hand, if I were made to feel needed—yeah. That would do it. Rebecca stopped. This was really weird. She was trying to outsmart herself. It was very unsettling.

"You just have to tell her that you can't do it without her. You need her to organize her friends—you know they'll listen to her. After all, they hardly know you. Just make it clear that you *need* her help."

"Right," said Catherine.

When she was gone, Rebecca turned to Lewis. "Is it possible, do you think? One little action like this—do you really think it could change things?"

Lewis looked at her. "It could," he said. "But how it will change things—that's what we have to worry about."

CHAPTER TWENTY-SIX

Jonathon was standing in a wasteland. He was all alone. The trees were brown, dead. The grass was yellow. There was a lake but it was covered in green algae. The sun beat down on his head. He was thirsty. Terribly thirsty. But he couldn't drink the water—he knew that. There was no shelter from the sun. There was no food. A girl appeared, a girl with short brown hair and brown eyes. She was standing close to him but he couldn't speak to her. His mouth was too dry. She handed him a flask with water in it, but he was too weak to grasp it.

Then he woke up.

Jonathon stared at the ceiling. He needed a drink of water. Badly. Still caught up in the dream, he made his way to the bathroom, turned on the small water fountain attached to the tap, and took a long drink of pure cool water. This had to stop. These dreams had to stop.

He thought back to yesterday. He had told his great-grandmother about the time machine. She had looked at him, a smile on her face, and said, "Finally." That's all. Just "finally." He had tried to get her to talk about it, but she wouldn't. Then he'd asked her again about his dreams. "That machine," she had said, "may be able to help you. Remember a hundred years ago." That was all she'd say.

Jonathon had known from the moment he saw the time machine that it meant something to him. He had to see it again. He was going to go back to the museum.

He was just passing the apple tree on his way to his skimmer, when he stopped abruptly. What am I doing? he thought. I mean, here I am, in a time where there is no violence, no poverty, no illness, everyone gets along with everyone else, everyone respects everyone else, and I'm running after a time machine. To do what? I can't learn anything from the past. It's disgusting. And the future is going to be just like this.

But then the dreams flashed into Jonathon's mind once more. Maybe I should go to the hospital, he thought, not to the museum. They could treat me there. Maybe great-grandmother doesn't know what she's talking about. She won't really tell me anything anyway.

He got into the skimmer and sat there silently for a moment. He wondered if he should program it for the hospital or his great-grandmother's, but instead he programmed it for the museum. He felt drawn there as if by a magnet, although he couldn't understand why.

The guide was, again, thrilled to see Jonathon. This time he took Jonathon on a tour of the inside of the time machine. The entranceway with its rounded ceiling was filled with computer controls, which ran all along the inner wall. At the end of this corridor was a door. It opened into a small white room, big enough for three grown people to stand comfortably.

"Do you know how the machine works?" Jonathon asked, even though he expected the guide to answer no.

"Yes," the man answered, to Jonathon's surprise, "however, we don't use it anymore."

"But," Jonathon said, "I *could* use it. I mean, if I wanted to."

"Well," said the guide, "of course, no one would stop you. You can do as you please, just like everyone else."

"Can I access the central computer from here?" Jonathan asked.

"Naturally," replied the guide, pointing to an access pod. His manner had changed, though, and he viewed Jonathan with definite disapproval.

"Then I will," said Jonathon. All information was available to everyone. One just had to take the time to find it. It took him only a short time to bring up the schematics and to transfer them to his own data device. Holding the diagrams in front of him, he went over all the access codes and the programming method. He was sure he could do it.

But why would he? And where and when would he go? He couldn't get over the thought that he was just being silly. He thanked the guide and left.

He programmed the skimmer for school. He could still take his afternoon classes. And he could get some lunch. He was hungry.

His school, which specialized in space studies, was on the outskirts of the city but still attached to the rest of the city structures. There was an open area for skimmers with a large green park beside it, plus a glass-covered area where space flights were simulated. He went in the back door and strode down the corridor to the central cafeteria. It was a big round room, with clear round tables and tall air chairs placed in a circular pattern. In the centre was a round lunch table with two robots that helped dole out the food. There were potted trees interspersed between the other tables. Each table had a small indentation in the centre in which flowering plants like African violets or azaleas were planted. Along the walls were holograms of nature scenes, like wheat fields waving in the wind, or scenes from space, such as an explosion of a supernova. The cafeteria was almost empty, as most classes were already in session. He knew it was rude to be late, but he just had to eat. He asked the robot for a soy burger with the works, a piece of cherry pie, and some fresh strawberry juice. The robot placed everything neatly on a bright pink tray.

"Thanks," Jonathon muttered.

"Hey, Jonathon!" It was Mark. Jonathon hadn't even noticed him. "Come on over."

Jonathon put his tray down at Mark's table and began to wolf down his food.

"Where've you been?" Mark asked, a smile on his face. "You're going to get behind."

"I know," Jonathon said, his mouth full. "Can I borrow your notes?"

"Sure."

"Why are *you* late?" Jonathon asked Mark, trying to get the conversation steered away from himself. He certainly didn't want to lie to one of his friends. But somehow he didn't want to tell Mark anything.

"'Well," Mark replied, "I've been working myself silly for the last month, and it's summer, and I know we have vacation soon, but I just got an urge to go for a swim. An uncontrollable urge," he grinned. "So I went. And then, of course, I was starving—I'm a growing thirteen-year-old, after all, so I had to have two soy burgers and three desserts. Well, I think I'm ready for class now."

"Yeah, me too, wait for me," Jonathon mumbled, stuffing the last of his burger in his mouth, taking a huge gulp of his drink, then cramming the pie in as fast as he could. "I'm coming with you."

The boys replaced their trays in the rack as they left and hurried to class. There were about twenty boys and girls in space class. Their teacher smiled at them as they entered. Everyone was at a computer console and the room was buzzing as students and computers conversed.

"We're planning a trajectory to Pluto," said Ms. Warren. "Want to give it a try?"

Mark answered with an enthusiastic yes; Jonathon tried to work up some excitement. He sat down at his computer. But instead of programming it to project his scientific data, he switched to a history mode, one almost never used, and he began to search for one hundred years ago. While the rest of the class worked on their Pluto trajectories, Jonathon sat spellbound as the history of that time unrolled before him. One item particularly intrigued him. On July 8, a girl called Rebecca Lepidus, her adopted brother and sister, Lewis and Catherine Lepidus, and Lonney Donnen led a group of Winnipeg students in a demonstration that was to have far-reaching effects. This demonstration was the first in a series which was to train young people in ways of effecting change. He gazed at the picture of the group. It was odd but they all seemed out of focus. The girl, Rebecca, reminded him of someone, but he couldn't think who it was...Jonathon thought he would like to join them, to see them making history. July 8. That was one hundred years ago tomorrow.

What was he thinking? He wasn't going to use the time machine. He didn't have to go anywhere. He didn't want to. He liked it right here. As for the dreams—well, he'd just have to learn to live with them. That was all. He'd insist that his great-grandmother tell him what she knew. If she wouldn't—well, fine.

CHAPTER TWENTY-SEVEN

"Rebecca, can I come in?"

"Not now, Cath, I'm busy."

"Rebecca, I really have to talk to you."

"Cath! I'm right in the middle...oh, come in!"

Rebecca sounded annoyed, so Catherine opened the door with caution, half expecting a book to land on her head as she entered.

"You know," said Rebecca, turning in her chair to face Catherine, "you were the one who got me into this. You and Lewis. Thanks to you, I'm spending my valuable summer studying. *Studying*! Okay, I know, I have to understand all this nuclear stuff before I can talk about it to other kids. So I try to spend a quiet evening working, and Mother gets impossible, you run in and out every five minutes about this protesting stuff—I mean, gimme a break."

Catherine picked her way through the clothes strewn all over the floor and sat down on Rebecca's bed. Catherine tried to ignore the mess. She hated anything that wasn't in perfect order. She also hated Rebecca's temper. As far as she was concerned, that was just another form of disorder. She had been taught to use logic to get her way, and she found that it worked for her. Rebecca, she thought, was often too emotional.

Catherine tried not to stare at Rebecca. It was so odd, to see her—again. She almost expected her to look different. It was strange to think that *this* Rebecca had no idea about there being two of her.

"Come on," said Rebecca, just as Catherine was ready to speak. "If we're going to talk, let's do it outside. I've been stuck up here all night and it's hot in here. A few minutes ago, I got a terrible headache all of a sudden and felt really dizzy. I'm okay now, but I could use some air."

"No, Rebecca!" exclaimed Catherine, but Rebecca was already past her on her way out of her room.

"Come on, Cath. I know how much you love to be outside," she called over her shoulder. "We'll just sit in the sunroom."

Catherine scrambled out of Rebecca's room and ran after her.

"No, Rebecca," she almost shrieked, "not the sunroom. It's a gorgeous night. I want to see the stars. Let's go out on the front lawn."

Rebecca had run down the stairs, and was heading into the living room. She stopped. "Okay," she said and followed Catherine out the front door and onto the front lawn. There were two medium-sized pine trees in the front yard, one on each side of the sidewalk leading to the house. They had been planted by Rebecca's dad as seedlings when they'd bought the house. The trees were a little closer to the street than to the house, so the girls flopped down on the lawn near the front steps and gazed up at the night sky.

Rebecca took a deep breath and sighed with delight. The air smelled of flowers and was warm on her skin, the sky was perfectly clear. Catherine slapped a mosquito that landed on her leg.

"There's something about you that they love," Rebecca remarked.

"Yes," said Catherine absently. "Now look, Rebecca," she said, trying to keep her voice calm, while her heart was still pounding at the thought of Rebecca almost running into herself in the sunroom, "uh, look, we really should go to this protest on Friday."

Rebecca was so delighted to be away from her books and was so enjoying the night air that she felt quite generous.

"Okay, Cath, tell me why it's so important."

"Because, Rebecca, pollutants in the air makes kids crazy. It hurts their brains. They can't function at school, they can't learn, they get wild...never mind the asthma and other stuff it causes."

Rebecca interrupted. "I know, Cath. You told me that already. But I mean why does it have to be *this* demonstration, right while we're trying to study and figure out this whole nuclear thing? I'd rather just focus on one issue at a time."

Catherine got up. "Because there's a meeting at City Hall on Friday afternoon. So if we make a big noise by picketing the factory on Friday morning, maybe we can get lots of parents out to the meeting on Friday afternoon."

Rebecca slapped a mosquito on her ear. "Oh no," she groaned, "I hate getting bitten there."

She slapped at another one on her foot "And there," she sighed. "The foot is the worst! We'd better go into the sunroom."

"No!" Catherine almost shouted.

Rebecca looked at her in surprise.

"Why not?"

"You know how I hate being cooped up," Catherine responded with a nervous laugh.

"No, I don't," Rebecca answered, looking at her friend quizzically.

"Well, I do. So let's stay out here. Now about the demonstration. I can't do it without you. I really need your help on this. If you could call Lonney and ask him to bring the rest of the kids from the peace group, we could all make some placards tomorrow and discuss strategy."

"Ouch!" yelled Rebecca. "I just punched myself in the nose trying to get that stupid mosquito. Ohhh, I'm going in."

"I'll go get the repellent," Catherine volunteered.

"No, the repellent is worse than the bites. It makes my tongue numb. Let's just go sit in the sunroom," and Rebecca was on her feet, walking round to the back of the house and the back door.

"Okay, Rebecca," Catherine yelled at the top of her lungs, "let's go into the sunroom."

"Catherine, are you crazy?" Rebecca turned and looked at her. "Why are you shouting?"

"I'm not shouting," Catherine objected as they reached the side of the house. "I'm just agreeing that we should *go into the sunroom!*"

Rebecca shook her head. Was everyone behaving strangely, or was it her imagination? She ran up to the back steps and waited for Catherine. But a sudden wave of nausea washed over her. She sat down heavily on the bottom step. Her head started to pound. Catherine sat down beside her on the step. Lewis opened the door to the sunroom, shut it quickly behind him, and walked down the steps to Rebecca.

"Shouldn't you be reading all that nuclear stuff?" he said to Rebecca.

Rebecca spluttered. "You're joking, I hope," she said.

"No."

"Well, yes, I should, if everyone would leave me alone!"

"Fine, we'll leave you alone," said Lewis.

"But will you come on Friday?" Catherine asked.

"Yes, yes, yes!" Rebecca exploded, leaping up. "I'll do it! I'll do everything! I'll study, I'll go to your meeting, I'll make posters—I don't have a life to call my own anymore! I'm just your stupid puppet!"

And she stalked back around the house, holding her head. Lewis and Catherine ran up the three steps and slipped back into the sunroom.

"That was too close," said Rebecca. "It made me feel sick again. But it goes away as soon as we're apart." She paused. "I've got quite a temper, don't I?"

"Yes," agreed Lewis, "you have."

"Still, I remember how I just wanted to get that work finished last week—without interruption!"

"You," stated Lewis, "can be very single-minded."

"And you can't?" Rebecca said.

"Now," said Catherine, trying to head off an argument, "we have to get you up to my room, Rebecca, without anyone seeing you. Come on. I'll go ahead. You go in between me and Lewis."

Catherine, with Rebecca and Lewis behind her, walked into the dining room and then the kitchen. No one was downstairs. Everything was quiet. *Click.* The outside door leading into the tiny vestibule off the kitchen opened and Rebecca's father walked in.

"Hi guys," he said, heading for the fridge "Nice outfit, Rebecca."

"Thanks, Dad," she answered, and they all rushed up the stairs, where they came face to face with Rebecca's mother at the top of the stairs. She had to stand to one side to let them pass. She looked at Rebecca's clothes. She looked up the stairs toward Rebecca's room. She opened her mouth to speak, then shook her head.

"I don't even want to know," she said, exasperated.

The kids passed her silently. Rebecca kept her head down, not daring to look at her mother for fear she'd blurt everything out. They hustled into Catherine's small room, so only a wall now divided the two Rebeccas.

Rebecca felt slightly sick, but it seemed that if the door was shut and the other Rebecca was in her room with her door shut, the feeling wasn't too severe. Anyway, she'd have to get used to it. She had nowhere else to go for the next two days.

CHAPTER
TWENTY-EIGHT

Rebecca awoke with a start. Where was she? Whose hand was pummelling her on her back? And who was knocking gently at the door?

"Rebecca," she heard Catherine hiss. "Rebecca, it's you. Get into the closet."

Oh yes, she was sleeping on the floor in Catherine's room. It was Catherine's hand. She heard another knock at the door.

"Oh my gosh," she murmured. She crawled over to the closet and squeezed herself in.

"Cath," called Rebecca, "it's time to get up. Mom says that since we're going to this thing on Friday we have to paint the house *today*. Great, eh? Although, I don't know, suddenly I feel really awful."

"You probably just need breakfast," called Catherine cheerfully. "I've never painted anything in my life," she added. "It might be fun. I'll be right down."

They could hear Rebecca moving away from the door.

Rebecca crawled out from the closet and leaned against the wooden frame of the bed. She had felt dizzy and nauseated while Rebecca was so close to the room. But the feeling eased as soon as Rebecca left.

"Ugh," Rebecca complained, "they're going to paint it that

horrible mustard colour." Then she remembered she couldn't go down for breakfast, which was even more depressing. "I'm starved. Can you smuggle me up some breakfast? You know," she mused, "it looks like my other self can't come near me either without feeling sick or weird."

"Makes sense," said Catherine, putting on a pair of jeans and an old shirt of Rebecca's that Rebecca had given her when Catherine had first arrived. "I'll get back up as soon as I can with some breakfast. Wait till we're all outside before using the bathroom."

"Right," sighed Rebecca, who didn't much like being a fugitive in her own house, stuck with nothing to do for two days.

"Cath," she said, "when the other Rebecca and I merge together, do you think I'll remember all the science that she's learned in the last two days?"

"I don't know," Catherine replied. "Maybe you will remember everything."

"Good," declared Rebecca, "then I'm going to find a good novel to read. No use in our both learning all that science." She grinned at Catherine.

Catherine slipped out the door, closing it quietly behind her.

Rebecca waited for what felt like hours until she heard the front door slam. Then she opened Catherine's door partway, poked her head out, and looked down the hall to the bathroom which was at the very end of the hall in between Lewis's room and her mom's study. There was no one in sight and she could hear no sounds. She bolted down the hall and into the bathroom.

So far, so good, thought Rebecca. She figured it would be okay to use her own toothbrush, and she couldn't resist taking a quick shower and washing her hair. She wrapped herself in a towel, snuck down the hall to her own room, grabbed a clean pair of shorts and a t-shirt, some socks and some underwear, a book off the shelf over her bed, and then darted back into Catherine's room to find a plate with bread, cheese, and a glass of orange juice.

I guess it would look suspicious, she thought, if Cath tried taking a bowl of Cheerios and milk upstairs. She sighed. This was better than nothing. She drank half the orange juice before getting dressed and had just polished off the bread and cheese when she noticed the damp towel in a heap on the rug. Better take that back, Rebecca thought, and she nipped out into the hallway again. When she returned from the bathroom, she plopped onto the bed, lying on her stomach, one hand holding the book, the other cupping her chin. Everything was quiet—a welcome change after the last few days. Not only that, but this time she got out of painting the house. She smiled to herself. There were some advantages to this situation.

Rebecca had just finished the fourth chapter of her novel when she heard everyone come inside. Most of the house was white stucco and they weren't going to paint that, so all they'd had to do was the front and side doors and the wooden siding on the front. Rebecca listened while they cleaned up, changed clothes, and went downstairs to eat lunch. Listening to them chatting over lunch made her feel lonely as well as hungry.

Then she heard Catherine volunteering to clean up after

lunch. A few minutes later Catherine was tapping on the door with her foot. Rebecca opened it to find Catherine with two leftover pieces of French toast from the frying pan and a glass of milk.

"Oh, yum," said Rebecca, seeing the French toast smothered in maple syrup. "Good thinking—offering to clean up like that!"

Catherine placed the food on her desk. "Don't make a mess!" she warned and hurried back downstairs to deal with the kitchen.

While Rebecca was upstairs enjoying her lunch, there was a knock at the kitchen door. Catherine opened it to find Lonney waiting on the steps.

"Hi, Cath," he said. "Thought I'd give you a hand with the posters."

"Good," she replied, smiling, "Lewis and Rebecca are in the basement. I'll be there as soon as I finish cleaning up here."

Lonney found Lewis and Rebecca hard at work painting a large poster which said "Lead or Life—your choice!" They were painting the words mustard yellow.

"Great colour," remarked Lonney instead of saying hello. He lifted his hand to show them where he'd gotten it on his knuckles when he knocked on the door.

"Yeah," said Rebecca, making a face, "I agree."

"Oh," said Lonney, "look at freckle face here!"

Rebecca stuck out her tongue at him. A few hours painting outside in the sun, and freckles had popped out all over her nose and cheeks.

Rebecca handed Lonney a brush. "Just get to work," she said.

"Sure thing—freckle face."

"Sticks and stones," replied Rebecca, and they both picked up their paint brushes and set to work. For the next couple of hours, the friends worked steadily, eagerly discussing their strategy for the rally.

Upstairs, the other Rebecca finally decided that she had no choice but to risk a trip to the bathroom. She peered down the hall and, seeing no-one, tiptoed toward the bathroom door. But as she was reaching for the handle, the door suddenly swung open and Lonney almost bowled her over.

"Hey," said Lonney, "I was just joking about your freckles, you know. You didn't have to put make-up on to cover them up. Really."

Rebecca stared at him, her heart pounding.

"Make-up?" she said, knowing he must be referring to the Rebecca he'd been sign-painting with downstairs. She was annoyed with herself for getting caught, even though Lonney didn't know he'd caught her.

"Uh, right, Lonney, I didn't put on make-up, they must've just faded," Rebecca mumbled as she rushed into the bathroom.

Lonney shrugged and wandered downstairs into the kitchen. A minute later, the other Rebecca joined him, having washed up in the little bathroom just off the front hall.

He laughed. "What did you do? Take off the make-up?"

"What?" she said.

"Take off the make-up—'cause I noticed you were trying to cover up your freckles? They're back again."

She looked at him strangely. "Don't you start, Lonney. You're one person I can depend on not to act crazy."

Now it was Lonney's turn to give Rebecca a strange look. But Rebecca's mom interrupted them by coming into the kitchen and asking Rebecca to set the table and help her with dinner.

"Well, I gotta go," said Lonney. "I'll see you tomorrow morning."

"Right," answered Rebecca, "see you then, freckles and all."

"Yeah," he called, on his way out. "Freckles and all."

"What was that all about?" asked her mom.

"Don't ask me," Rebecca answered. "Everyone around here is acting very strange." And she went to set the table.

CHAPTER TWENTY-NINE

The police were dressed in black—boots, pants, shirts, helmets with black plastic visors—and they were everywhere. Some were marching. Some were pushing men, women, even little children, one at a time, into a transparent, rectangular booth. The women were sobbing. One woman rushed at a guard. He shot her through the head, then threw her into the booth. One by one, the people walked into the booth. But no one came out. Once the person was inside, the guard activated the machine and the person was vaporized. Was that his mother? Yes, she was being shoved into the booth.

Jonathon screamed. The sound of his voice woke him up. He sat bolt upright, his eyes open.

A dream. Only a dream. Another dream.

But it all had something to do with the time machine. His great-grandmother had told him as much and pointed him to a certain year—and he had found an event he felt he just had to see.

He arrived at the museum and the guide looked at him with a mixture of respect and anxiety.

"So, you're determined to do it, young man," he remarked thoughtfully.

Jonathon nodded his head. "I have to."

"Where are you going to go?" asked the guide. "Ancient Rome? Egypt? The American frontier? England?"

"Winnipeg, exactly a hundred years ago," Jonathon answered. "I have to go there."

"I was wondering..." the guide began hesitantly. "Do you know who I am, son?"

"No."

"My name is Dr. Simcox. This is my machine. It was my trip that caused some...very nasty unintended consequences."

"Like what?" asked Jonathon.

"I'd rather not go into it," Dr. Simcox said. "Suffice it to say there are often unintended consequences to time travel."

"I—I have to do this," Jonathon stammered.

"Then I might as well help you," Dr. Simcox answered. "Don't want you materializing inside solid rock or ending up in the wrong time."

Jonathon hesitated. He had no guarantee that this time trip would stop his bad dreams. Why was he going? Why did he feel so compelled to do this?

"Change your mind?" asked the doctor.

"No, no," Jonathon replied, although his words didn't sound too convincing.

"You'll need this." Dr. Simcox took a small black box from its pinning on the wall. "It's the transmitter. Don't lose it. You'll need it to get back." He pointed to the digital display. "See? We'll set it for 0, that's Winnipeg, 40 N.E. Unless you specifically change the date when you activate it, you'll return on that date and time in the past to the same date and time in our present. For instance, it's set for July 8, one hundred years ago. If you stay one day, July 9 will then show on the readout. Activate the machine and you'll arrive here, July 9, 40."

Dr. Simcox went to work. Jonathon watched him, feeling almost numb. He could still change his mind, couldn't he?

Dr. Simcox was working with speed and assurance. Finally he stopped, surveyed the digital displays, and turned to Jonathon.

"It's ready. Are you?"

Jonathon found that he couldn't speak. He nodded his head. Slowly, feeling as if he were in one of his dreams, Jonathon walked toward the door of the time-travel dome. Dr. Simcox pushed a small button and the door slid up. Jonathon walked inside. The door closed. He stared at the smooth curved walls.

That's when the panic set in. Jonathan opened his mouth to shout, to tell Dr. Simcox to stop, when the walls softened and dissolved into a white blur.

Suddenly there was a terrible blare, then screeching, and shouts all around him. He put his hands to his ears and looked around. He was surrounded by vehicles. They were driving on the ground and they were making a terrible noise. People were leaning out of their vehicles shouting at him. A man dressed in some kind of a blue uniform appeared at his side, took his arm, and moved him out of the way of the vehicles to a walkway crowded with people hustling past.

"What got into you?" the man said sternly, looking down at him.

"I don't know," Jonathon answered, his voice shaking. "It was a mistake," he added, not knowing what else to say.

"Another mistake like that and you'll be dead," said the man. He walked off, leaving Jonathon alone.

Jonathon looked around. Vehicles whizzed past. Weren't they called *cars* in those days? On either side of the walkway was a building made out of some kind of white material. One building was higher than the other. Across the street was another structure with "Museum of Man and Nature" written in big letters on the outside. Of course! The new museum had been built right near the site of the old one. He was here! He'd made it. He looked around at the four lanes of cars, felt the heat, and coughed.

What was the matter with the air? He looked up. The sky was blue, the sun was shining. But the sky was not the blue he was used to, there was a slight grey tinge in it. And the air—it smelled terrible and it made his chest feel tight. People were rushing past him as if in a terrible hurry, except for some who lined up near the road behind a sign with numbers written on it, blank expressions on their faces, waiting. For what, he wondered? He turned to look at the building behind him. His whole body was tingling as if it had electricity running through it. His eyes sparkled. He shook his long red hair and noticed some older people staring at him.

He was really here! What should he do first?

CHAPTER THIRTY

A large vehicle stopped on the other side of the street. When it pulled away, Jonathon saw that about twenty kids had gotten out of it. They were laughing, talking, shouting, and carrying huge signs. They crossed the street, almost where he was standing, and then headed for one of the buildings behind him. One sign said "Lead or Dead?" and another said "Get the Lead Out!" What were they doing? What did this mean? Was this the demonstration he'd read about? As they hurried past him, he could feel their excitement. No one really noticed him; they were too busy talking amongst themselves. Jonathon decided to follow them.

The walkway opened out into a courtyard between two buildings. There was a fountain in the centre of the courtyard and Jonathon could feel a fine mist on his face as the wind carried the water away from its source. The kids turned into the building closest to them. Jonathon followed them inside to a series of grey steps. The building was cool and the air smelled fresh after the heat and odours of the outdoors. The kids ran up the steps and he ran up with them, following the group into a large auditorium. Many of the seats were already filled with adults. In the centre was a pit with long tables and chairs and more adults. The adults in the pit did not seem happy. They glared at the kids, who were still making a lot of noise, chatting and laughing as they were getting settled.

Jonathon sat behind a boy and a girl. The girl had hair as red as his own, the boy had hair as long as his. The seats were filling up. Another girl sat down beside him and tapped the red-headed girl in front of them on the shoulder.

"Happy, Catherine?" the girl asked.

The redhead turned around. "Yes," she beamed, "and thanks for coming."

"No, you were right—we were right to come." The second girl turned to Jonathon and grinned.

Jonathon's heart almost stopped beating. It was the girl from his dreams! Short brown hair, brown eyes, freckles—oh yes, he'd know that face anywhere! His great-grandmother had been right. There were answers for him here.

"Were you at the demonstration?" the girl asked him. "I didn't see you. Great, wasn't it? I'll bet every newspaper in the country will have a story on this."

"What's your name?" asked Jonathon, forcing his voice to sound normal, relaxed.

"I'm Rebecca," she replied.

"Lepidus?" he asked.

"Yes," she answered, surprised. "How do you know?"

"And this must be the anti-pollution demonstration," said Jonathon slowly.

"Well, yes," she said. "Weren't you there?"

"No," he answered, "I just arrived. You're right though. It will be in every newspaper. Then things will die down, but you and your group will keep going. This is your first training session for what's to come. Oh boy, do you realize what you've done today?"

"Oh, I don't know," she laughed. "We've tried to help some families who are stuck living next to this factory—that's all."

"No, you've done more than that," Jonathon said. There was so much he wanted to ask her, but he didn't want to scare her off. The girl in his dreams was Rebecca Lepidus, the girl who had helped shape his future. Why had he dreamt about her? And why had his great-grandmother directed him to this time and place?

"Ssshhh, Rebecca, pipe down. The council is discussing the factory."

Rebecca gave Jonathon a puzzled look. "What's your name?" she whispered.

"Jonathon Kobrin."

"Where do you live?"

"Winnipeg."

"Where in Winnipeg?"

"Oh, the south end of the city."

"Yeah? Me, too. What school do you go to?"

Now he was stumped.

"Ssshhh," he whispered, "I want to hear this." He had to have time to think. What could he tell her?

The meeting went on and on. Everyone wanted to talk. Some said the factory would close if they were forced to install expensive equipment to reduce emissions and then all the workers would lose their jobs. Others said that the company could afford it but just didn't want to lower their profit margin. Jonathon soon lost track of all the arguments.

This was it. The beginning. A little demonstration that the newspapers thought was cute—a bunch of kids trying to do something—so the newspapers played it up. Which gave other kids ideas, and they started nuclear protests and other environmental demonstrations—and the children's movement continued and grew stronger and more forceful as they grew older. And, well, Jonathon was living with the results. He sighed. If only he knew how she would react if he tried to tell her the truth. Somehow, he felt there was something familiar about her. It was the same feeling he had in his dreams.

"What's the matter?" Rebecca whispered.

"Nothing," he said. "You wouldn't understand."

"What were you talking about before?" She persisted. "You seem to think you know how this'll all turn out."

"You wouldn't believe me," he said.

"Try me."

A crooked smile crossed his face. What did he have to lose?

"Because I'm from the future and I know how it all happens."

"But...what about—" she stared at him.

The next moment, everyone was clapping.

"We did it!" said the redhead, turning to Rebecca.

"What? I didn't hear," Rebecca admitted distractedly, still staring at Jonathon.

"They have one year to get the emissions down thirty percent. Two years, fifty percent. Three years, seventy-five percent!"

"That's great, Cath," Rebecca said. Then she looked at Jonathan with an odd expression on her face. "Look, I'd like you to meet Jonathon."

"Hi," said Catherine, beaming.

At that point another boy stood up and turned to them. He looked at Jonathon curiously.

"Lewis," said Rebecca, "this is Jonathon."

"Hello," said Lewis.

"Jonathon says he's from the future," Rebecca stated.

Lewis and Catherine almost seemed to stop breathing. They looked at Jonathon, then at Rebecca.

"You don't, by any chance," said Catherine slowly, "have a sister named Tara, do you?"

Now it was Jonathon's turn to freeze. For a moment he was quite speechless.

"Yes," he said finally. "Yes, I do. But how do you know that?"

"How would you like to come home with Lewis, Rebecca, and me?" Catherine asked. "So we can talk."

"Well, yes, I'd like that," Jonathon replied. He couldn't believe his luck. They were inviting him to go with them! He'd be able to get to the bottom of this Rebecca business, he just knew it. He looked at Rebecca, whose eyes were darting back and forth between Catherine and Lewis.

"Who's Tara?" she asked them.

"My sister," Jonathan said.

"And you knew that *how*?" she asked Cath and Lewis.

"Lucky guess," said Lewis.

"Everyone has been acting very weird," said Rebecca, "and now here's someone else from the future, but it can't be..." She paused. "What's going on?"

"I think Jonathan should tell us that," Cath said.

"Sure," he said, though he wondered briefly what Rebecca could have meant by *someone else*. "I'll tell you everything you'd like to know."

CHAPTER
THIRTY-ONE

"There's the bus, there's the bus!" cried Rebecca, running ahead of them.

Lewis had taken Jonathon's arm and had a firm hold of it, seemingly determined not to let Jonathon out of his sight.

Jonathon was wondering how they could have known about Tara. It was one thing for *him* to know the *past*, but quite another for *them* to know the *future*. On the other hand, only Catherine and Lewis had mentioned Tara, and Rebecca didn't seem to know what they were talking about.

Maybe Catherine and Lewis had supernatural powers—or something. And he still couldn't believe he was here with the girl from his dreams, a real flesh-and-blood girl.

Jonathon was pulled up the steps of the vehicle they called a "bus" and Lewis sat him down next to Rebecca. He looked around with interest. Not that different from the large air skimmers we use to transport people back and forth to their ecological stations, he thought. Except much bumpier and dirtier and older. He looked out the windows.

"Want to trade seats?" Rebecca asked. She was sitting by the window.

"Thank you," Jonathon answered, and they switched. There were some very tall buildings looming to his left. He craned his neck.

"They're so high," he whispered.

"I thought you said you were from Winnipeg," Rebecca said.

"I am, I am," he muttered. "What is that?"

"That's a hotel," she replied.

"How many layers does it have?" he asked.

"*Layers*? I don't know." She seemed to smile at his use of the word "layers."

The bus turned down Portage Avenue. Jonathon stared at the shop windows filled with goods to sell, some with racks of clothes displayed on the sidewalks in front of the stores.

The buildings were all many layers high and mostly square. They were ugly. The sharp angles, the drab colours, the grey roads: it was all horrible. When the bus turned down Memorial Drive, Jonathon caught a glimpse of an interesting structure.

"What's that?" he asked Rebecca.

"It's the art gallery."

Jonathon looked at her. He liked her. She obviously didn't know what to make of him, but at least she was giving him a chance.

Just then he caught sight of a golden statue perched

atop a large building set in the middle of lots of grass and trees. Why, he'd seen it standing in a corner of the museum. Covered in dust. It held a torch up with one arm and a sheaf of wheat under the other arm.

"The Golden Boy," Rebecca told him.

Jonathon was just about to ask Rebecca about the Golden Boy and tell her how pretty the parks looked, when they drove over the Osborne Street Bridge and he saw the river.

"Oh!" he exclaimed. "What's wrong with the river?"

Rebecca looked out the window. "Nothing," she answered. She loved the river. The trees leaning over the water were in full bloom, a small boat drifted downstream. Everything looked peaceful to her, beautiful.

"It's so ugly."

"Ugly? What do you mean?"

"Well, it's a funny colour. It's not the colour it should be. It's sort of brown. And no one's swimming in it."

Rebecca looked at Jonathon in astonishment.

"Of course no one swims in it," she replied, "or hardly anyone. It's too dirty. It's polluted. I guess you're right about the colour, but that's from the mud."

Jonathon continued to stare out the window. They drove past the Osborne Street stop, then turned onto Corydon Avenue.

Jonathon pointed to the apartment buildings.

"What are those?"

"Apartments," Rebecca answered.

"What are apartments?"

"Why," she paused. "There are lots of little separate living quarters in those buildings. People pay money to live there."

"Oh yes," said Jonathon, "I've heard about money. But I'd hate to live so high up. I'd feel all closed in."

Finally they were getting to the residential section of River Heights where Rebecca lived.

"Come on," she said to Jonathon, "it's time to get off."

He followed her off the bus, Lewis and Catherine right behind them. They crossed Corydon, walked past a school and a library, and then down a street until they reached Rebecca's house.

Jonathon looked at the white-and-mustard-coloured two-storey home, with the two fir trees in front.

"It's prettier here," he said. "Much nicer." He looked with approval at the large trees lining the streets, their branches almost meeting in the centre of the road.

Lewis and Catherine ran up the front stairs ahead of Rebecca and Jonathon.

"We just have to go upstairs for a while," Catherine said. "We'll meet you in the sunroom."

"Sure," Rebecca agreed, and she led Jonathon into the house.

There was a note on the kitchen table which Rebecca picked up and read.

"My dad is out playing tennis and Mom has gone to the library. So I guess it's just us kids. Can I get you something to eat?" she asked Jonathon.

"Yes, please," he replied, and followed her into the kitchen, curious to taste some food from the past.

* * *

Lewis and Catherine burst into Catherine's room, almost scaring Rebecca to death.

She dropped her book.

"What's the matter with you two?" she said. Even Lewis looked flustered.

Lewis shut the door. He sat down on the only chair in the room. Catherine sat on the bed next to Rebecca.

"Jonathon is here," Catherine said dramatically.

Rebecca looked at her, not understanding. "Jonathon who?"

"Jonathon," Lewis repeated, his voice taking on a pained tone, as if he were lecturing a three-year-old. "Jonathon. *Your* Jonathon. *From-the-future* Jonathon. The one who has a sister named Tara."

Rebecca looked at them, bewildered. "Come on, guys," she said. "He can't be here. You know he's coming tomorrow, and he's coming to Assiniboine Park—if he comes at all."

"He's here!" Catherine insisted. "Downstairs. With you. He told you that he was from the future. We're supposed to go on down now and hear the whole story."

Rebecca looked at them closely. They seemed sincere. Lewis, after all, hardly even knew what a joke was. She didn't like the sound of this. Not at all. She began to bite her thumbnail. On the one hand, she felt terribly relieved: He was here. But on the other hand, she was terribly worried. It was the wrong day.

"He can't be here now. It throws off our whole plan. How will I ever get back to being one again? And how on earth," she added, "did he just happen to bump into you guys?"

"We don't know," said Lewis, "but we're going down to the sunroom to find out."

"I'm coming, too," Rebecca declared, scrambling off the bed.

"Oh no, you're not," Lewis ordered. "The other Rebecca is there. Don't you remember what happens to you when you get close to her?"

Rebecca sighed. She sat down.

"All right," she said.

"We'll come right back up," Catherine assured her, "and tell you what he says." They left the room.

Rebecca sat on the bed. Jonathon *here*. But was it him? Only she could answer that question. Only she had ever seen him. And if it was him, what was he saying? What was he telling them?

She couldn't stand it. She had to find out. She got off the bed and quietly opened Catherine's door. She poked her head out. All quiet. She ran to the top of the stairs. Still all quiet. Slowly, she started down the stairs. When she reached the bottom step, she could hear the murmur of conversation coming from the sunroom.

Rebecca decided to approach the group through the living room/dining room, instead of the kitchen. She crawled so they couldn't see her through the sunroom windows. The dining room door that led into the sunroom was open. She crouched behind it. A wave of nausea swept over her. Was she going to be sick?

"It's so different where I come from," said a familiar voice. Very carefully, slowly, she peeked around the door. There he was, sitting at the small white table, with Lewis, Catherine and, yes, her freckled self.

Slam! The front door banged shut.

"Hi! I'm home." It was her mother. If she didn't move fast, her mother would soon see her and then her double. What a mess! Why hadn't she stayed in her room? She crawled away from the door, still on all fours. Her nausea subsided as she got farther away from the sunroom. Her mother walked into the living room.

"Looking for something?" her mother asked.

"Uh, yeah, uh, Marta called and said she'd lost an earring. One of her little pearls."

"Oh dear," said her mom. "I vacuumed down here this morning while you were all out. Maybe you'd better check the bag."

"Ugh," groaned Rebecca. "Okay. But I'll phone her first to see if it's shown up."

"Who's in the sunroom?" asked her mom.

"The sunroom?" repeated Rebecca, her voice coming out high and squeaky. "Oh, just Lewis and Cath and some kids. You know, from the demonstration."

"I'll just go say hello."

"No! I mean…that is…I really need your help right now. Some of this science stuff is really hard to understand. I mean, what do they mean by 'rate of erosion,' anyhow?" She scrambled to her feet, grabbed her mother's hand, and pulled her upstairs.

"Now, where is it?" Rebecca said, rummaging around on her desk, looking for her science book.

"Listen, darling, come show me when you've found it. I'm really thirsty. I'm going to get a soda water."

"But, Mom!"

"I'll just be in the kitchen." Her mother stopped. "Your freckles faded quickly, didn't they?" Then she walked out.

Rebecca sank onto her bed. Now what? It seemed as if the only thing she could do was to go back into hiding. Lewis and Catherine would have to sort this out. She went back into Catherine's room and shut the door, dreading to think what her mother would say when she saw the other Rebecca downstairs.

CHAPTER
THIRTY-TWO

Rebecca paced up and down the small floor of Catherine's room. What was she doing cooped up like this? She felt like a caged animal. Jonathon was here. Jonathon. She had just said goodbye to him a few days ago. And now, everything was different. He wouldn't know her yet. She had to talk to him. The other Rebecca didn't know anything. She was furious with herself for not insisting on being the one to have gone to the demonstration. After all, she was the one who really understood what was at stake. Most of all, she wanted to talk to Jonathan.

The door opened. Catherine slipped in and stood with her hands on her hips.

"Sit down. I can hear you walking around from downstairs. We can't afford to have you found out!"

"Why not?" Rebecca exploded. "I'm sick of this. That's *Jonathon* down there. I have to talk to him! We have to tell him everything. This is all getting out of control."

"Calm down, Rebecca. Actually, I think you're right. He'll have to be brought into our confidence. I'll try to get him away from the other Rebecca and bring him up here. Then we'll see."

"Fine," said Rebecca, still feeling angry. "Do that."

Catherine glared at her and left the room.

Rebecca sat and bit her nails. And waited.

Finally the door opened.

"Your mother came to the rescue," said Catherine, entering first. "She sent the other you to the drugstore for some more Tylenol. She got a headache when she saw you downstairs after just seeing you upstairs. Lewis and I insisted that Jonathon stay here with us. Here he comes. We haven't told him anything," she added in a whisper.

Lewis ushered Jonathon into Catherine's room. Jonathon looked at Rebecca.

"I thought you went to a store for drugs," he said.

Rebecca felt quite overcome at seeing him. She smiled weakly.

"That's a drugstore," she corrected him, "Oh, never mind— anyway, it wasn't me."

"Yes, it was," Jonathon insisted. "I just saw you go."

"Look," Rebecca said urgently, "the drugstore is only a fifteen-minute walk away. We've got maybe half an hour to talk before she gets back."

"She?" Jonathon interrupted. "Oh!" he exclaimed. "I see. You're twins!"

Lewis and Catherine shook their heads. Lewis spoke. "Jonathon, they are not twins. I think you'd better listen to Rebecca."

Rebecca proceeded to tell Jonathon about their previous meeting. About his taking her to his future. What that future was like. And her early arrival back home.

When she was finished there was a very long silence. Jonathon didn't seem to be able to speak. His face had turned an ashen grey. Finally he spoke.

"I dreamt it all," he said, his voice cracking.

"What?" Rebecca said.

"I dreamt it all," he repeated. "I dreamt about you. I saw this 'Zanu,' this future. I was always in trouble and you were always there. The dreams got so bad that I felt I was going crazy. But my time is nothing at all like that one! My great-grandmother sent me to the museum. She seemed to know a lot—she sort of pointed me to you—well, to this year anyway—and then I discovered the demonstration and..." He looked at the three of them.

Jonathon smiled at Rebecca. His whole face lit up. Rebecca thought he looked as if the weight of the world had been lifted off him.

"This is unbelievable," Jonathon said to her. "You've been to a different future and you've met me and I was an underground fighter—am I still there? Is the future that you saw still there? Separate from us? Or have you changed everything and there's only one future, the one I've been living in?"

"I don't know," answered Rebecca. "Your friend Mark told me that the future is like a fan, with endless ribs, and that what I saw were possible futures, separate timelines. I guess the one you've come from is another timeline—one that we're making. One that we began to create today with the demonstration. I wish I could see it."

CHAPTER
THIRTY-THREE

Rebecca stared at her freckles in the mirror that hung over her vanity table. If only there weren't so many of them, she thought. And today was the picnic, so she'd get even more. The other kids would tease her. As she brushed her hair, she pondered the simple, blunt cut with the part at the side. Maybe she should grow her hair and wear bangs, let her hair fall all over her face, or dye it green. That would draw attention away from her freckles. Maybe her bright red shorts and t-shirt would help.

She would have to run all those stupid races at the picnic. But at least Jonathon was coming. Lewis had hidden him in his room last night, then Jonathon had snuck outside and rung the doorbell at eight this morning, pretending to be a friend they had met at the demonstration.

Jonathan had told Rebecca he was anxious to compete in the races. He said he'd never competed in his life. They didn't believe in competition where he came from. Where he came from. Oh, how she longed to see his future. She'd asked him several times yesterday to take her, and again this morning at breakfast, but he kept saying maybe later.

But she had a plan. He could take her to his present and she could see her future for herself, maybe even look in the history books and find out what she'd done that was so important, so she could be sure to do it, and then she'd come back here. Also, she wanted to make sure she was changing things for the better. Jonathon said everything was perfect, but his idea of perfect and hers might be very different.

She knew that he carried the transmitter in his pocket. He had shown it to her. If she could just get him to take it out, show it to her, maybe she could activate it and—he'd be furious, of course, but he'd cool down again. And then maybe he'd give her a grand tour of the future. Yes, she definitely wanted to see how all this was going to turn out. It would be so much easier if he'd just cooperate.

* * *

Rebecca sat at Catherine's vanity table and brushed her hair. Her face was so pale, she looked like she'd been cooped up for weeks, not days. But, she supposed, the idea of disappearing would make anyone pale. She picked up Catherine's brush and pulled it through her hair. She looked at the red shorts and red t-shirt she was wearing. She knew it was the same colour that her other self was wearing—she'd insisted Catherine tell her. Her mother had seen them on sale and, not being able to resist a bargain, had bought two pairs exactly the same. At the time, Rebecca had complained; red was not even her favourite colour. But now they'd become part of her plan.

Lewis and Catherine had both come in to talk to her. They agreed with Jonathon. They thought that she should just relax and vanish, that it would be painless and, in fact, necessary. They were so logical. Yes, maybe it was the logical solution. But didn't they understand how she felt? They kept saying, "But the other

Rebecca *is* you. You won't be dying. You'll just go back to being one." But she'd had all these new experiences—like the trip to Zanu. They'd be wiped out. Wasn't that a kind of death? It felt that way to her. She felt so alone and friendless. She had no one to turn to.

But she had a plan. She'd go to the picnic, too. She'd watch. She'd wait. She had to get Jonathon alone. Then she'd grab that transmitter. If she went into the future at the same time as before, she might survive. It was, at least, a chance. It was better than doing nothing. What that would do to the future she didn't know. Maybe she'd end up back in Zanu. All she was concerned about at the moment was her survival. She could come back and go to lots of demonstrations and peace marches and still change things. She knew that. But first she had to survive. After all, only she knew about Zanu—what they had to avoid. That other Rebecca was ignorant in comparison to her. Practically stupid.

* * *

Rebecca and Jonathon were alone in a small clearing surrounded by willow trees. Everyone else had gone to the pavilion for ice cream. Rebecca had said she was too tired—but would they please bring her an ice cream and one for Jonathon, too? She wanted him to stay and keep her company.

"I wish I could see your future," she said as they lay on their backs, looking up at the sky.

"Please, Rebecca," said Jonathon, "don't start that again. I'm not ready to go yet. And when I do, I don't really want to take you. You don't have to go into the future. It could just complicate things more. Besides, when you get back to your own time, wouldn't you just feel like a puppet? Like you had no more say in your own future?"

"But I'm *dying* to see your present."

And she reached over and gave him a playful tickle in the ribs.

He laughed. "Hey, don't."

"Don't what?" she said, all innocence, as she sat up and tickled him again.

"Don't!" he exclaimed, rolling over on his side, laughing.

"Don't what?" she repeated and tickled him again, this time grabbing for the transmitter in his pocket.

She had it in her hand. She pulled it out of his pocket and jumped up and away from him.

* * *

Rebecca was hiding behind a huge willow, watching the other Rebecca and Jonathon. They were lying on their backs, talking. She had to get her hands on that transmitter. Wait a minute. What was the other Rebecca doing? She was tickling Jonathon. That is not like me, uh, her, Rebecca thought. I, uh, she doesn't know him well enough. She is up to something. What a schemer. I'm not sure I like her all that much. No, I don't like the look of this at all.

The other Rebecca had something in her hand. Jonathon was angry. He was yelling. She was holding it up. Oh my gosh. It had to be the transmitter. The other her was going to use it. And when she does, Rebecca thought, perhaps I won't exist. Or perhaps she'll go off and leave me here. Intact. The survivor. What should I do? Rebecca had never felt so indecisive in her life. Her very self was at stake. Somehow she felt that she could not let herself be left behind. Whatever her other self was doing, she had to do it, too.

* * *

Rebecca held the transmitter tightly in one hand, the index finger of her other hand hovering over the red button. She just had to press down...

"Stop!"

Rebecca looked up. Someone burst out of the willow thicket. She was wearing red shorts and a red t-shirt.

It was...*her*.

Rebecca was so shocked that the transmitter slipped from her hand and fell to the ground. A terrible wave of nausea washed over her. The image didn't speak to her but kept running, slowly, as if she was having trouble lifting her legs. Now she was going for the transmitter. So was Jonathon. Rebecca had to get it back. But her head hurt so much she could barely see.

All three of them lunged for the transmitter. There was a huge crashing noise as if the air itself was being rent open. Someone must have pressed the button. White light flashed around them, electrical currents slashed the air, and then everything was quiet.

CHAPTER THIRTY-FOUR

Rebecca's head felt like it was about to explode. All the experiences of the past few days were meeting, racing through her, becoming memories. Had she really been two people? Yes, she thought, she had, and now she was one. It had worked. She remembered everything: the trip to Zanu, being sent back too early, hiding in Catherine's room. She also remembered going to the demonstration, wondering why everyone was behaving so strangely, planning to grab the transmitter and come into the future. She felt tears trickling down her cheeks. She had felt so sorry for herself, shut up in Catherine's room, alone, afraid, no one to help her. I should have come to me, she thought. Why didn't I? The two of us could have worked it out. But then she remembered the nausea. And there had been a terrible shock when her two selves met, but they—she—had survived. Perhaps because they had gone into the future together, it hadn't caused the kind of terrible changes that Lewis had worried about. Or she hoped it hadn't. She felt so odd. All the memories were so fresh, she still felt she had two separate people inside her.

She and Jonathon were sitting on a floor. Jonathon was staring at her.

"I'm back together, Jonathon!" Rebecca exclaimed. "I don't know how, but I'm back together."

Rebecca looked around. They were in a small white room. It reminded her of the time capsule that had originally taken her to the future.

"Jonathon, this may be hard for you to understand, but when I grabbed the transmitter from you it was—well, I just *had* to. I felt drawn here. Like I had to see this. And the other me was scared—scared of dying."

Jonathon considered this for a moment. "I understand," he replied. "I felt drawn to your time for some reason—and drawn to you, too. I don't know why. I mean, I even dreamt about you. How is that possible?"

Rebecca shook her head. "I can't explain it either. It doesn't seem logical to me."

"Not everything can be explained with logic," a voice said.

Jonathon and Rebecca turned toward the voice. Dr. Simcox was standing in the doorway. "So," he smiled, "did everything go all right?"

Jonathon smiled back.

"Yes, thank you. This is a friend of mine from the past. Her name is Rebecca Lepidus."

Dr. Simcox raised his eyebrows. "Really?" he said. "Interesting."

"Hi," said Rebecca.

"Welcome," he replied. "Well, now what do you two intend to do?"

"Go see my great-grandmother," Jonathon replied, without a moment's hesitation. "I've got to tell her everything."

"Actually, she's been here," Dr. Simcox said.

"What?" exclaimed Jonathon. "What was she doing here?"

"Well, she seemed to know that you'd gone and wanted me to give you a message."

"What message?" Jonathon asked, looking quite bewildered.

"She said you should take Rebecca on a tour. Give her a sense of our world. When you've done that, go to her house."

Jonathon shook his head. "But how could she know that I was bringing Rebecca back? How did she know I was going? I didn't tell her."

"I can't answer that," Dr. Simcox replied. "But I believe you should follow her suggestion."

Jonathon and Rebecca got to their feet. "How about it?" Jonathon said. "Want to see some of your future?"

"Would I!" exclaimed Rebecca.

"Well, then," Jonathon smiled. "Let's go. Thanks for everything, Dr. Simcox. We'll see you again soon."

"I know you will," he replied. "She can't stay here forever."

"No," Rebecca laughed. "I'd like to get back home at some point. And this time all in one piece."

Jonathon took Rebecca's hand and led her out of the time machine and through the museum. She got a fleeting glimpse of the exhibits, but they were soon out in the skimmer lot. The sky was a clear deep blue. The air was even purer than the air at her parents' cottage at Falcon Lake. She took a deep breath. Jonathon did, too.

"Now that smells good," he sighed, looking pleased, even contented. "Here's my skimmer."

It wasn't that different, Rebecca thought, from the skimmers in Zanu. Silvery-blue on the outside, blue-grey on the inside, just enough room for five people. The dash was fully computerized, the seats somehow soft and yet firm.

"What are the seats made of?" she asked Jonathon as she settled in.

"Air," he replied. "Like them?"

"Mmmm," she sighed, "yes."

"Well," said Jonathon, "where to first? I know. I'll show you Winnipeg. Then we'll go to my home. We'll sleep there tonight. And tomorrow—we'll go wherever you want. Just tell me and we'll plan it tonight." As he spoke the skimmer lifted off the ground.

"Anywhere?" Rebecca asked.

"Anywhere," Jonathon answered.

"Like anywhere in Canada?"

"We don't have a Canada anymore. We can go anywhere in the world. We just have to reserve space on a transit. Or we could book into a tour."

"Wow!" Rebecca stared below her. "It's beautiful!"

"We like it," Jonathon beamed.

She looked at him. "You look—really glad to be home," she remarked.

He grinned. "It's funny," he replied. "But you're right. I don't know why, but I feel wonderful. Like a terrific weight has been lifted off my shoulders."

"So do I," she laughed. "I feel—just great! Here I am in the future, a future I helped make somehow, and I'm going to get to see it. *And* I'm in one piece again!" She laughed again. Her eyes were sparkling. "I feel wonderful!"

"Let's see," said Jonathon. "Where to first? I know—I'll show you our community centres." He put the skimmer down in a large lot. Rebecca followed him through a sliding door and into a central foyer. It was round with gleaming wood floors and wood walls.

"We use wood, as you do," Jonathon explained, "but we never cut down a tree without replacing it with another. The rainforests survived because people eventually stopped cutting them down. Now we have wood harvest lots, and cutting and replacement are carefully monitored. We also use a lot of bamboo because it grows so quickly." He took her in a small elevator to the lower level. There was a large, round swimming pool with a smaller one for little children, change rooms, hot tubs, and saunas. On the main level there was a daycare facility that included a large gym, equipped with climbing structures, slides, mats, and lots of room for running, and another room used for exercising and dancing. He also showed her a medical facility on the same floor, where people were advised on diet and wellness, and three game rooms for children under the age of fifteen. The games were holograms—games of skill, dream visualizations, and three-dimensional video games. There were a few kids playing in each of the rooms. They all greeted Jonathon and Rebecca, and invited them to play.

"This is incredible," Rebecca said as Jonathon took her from one activity to the next. "And you say there's one of these centres for every hundred houses?"

"Yes," Jonathon replied.

"It's great you have all this stuff for kids to do," Rebecca said.

"It's great that it's available to everyone—not just people who can afford it."

"Kids are very important people here," Jonathan said. "Maybe smaller people, but people. It's crucial that every child is given every opportunity to develop—in every way. We kids do things ourselves," he added. "We run most of our own programs."

"Except the daycare," Rebecca laughed.

"Yes," Jonathon agreed, "but the older kids help out there, too. Or those of us who like little kids, anyway."

The rest of the afternoon was a whirl of activity. They saw restaurants, art galleries, theatres. They went for a half-hour boat ride on the Red River—which was so clean and beautiful Rebecca couldn't even recognize it, although it still retained its brown colour, from the mud at the bottom. Finally they arrived at Jonathon's house, just in time for dinner.

Jonathon looked quite sheepish when he walked in. "Mom! Dad! I'm home."

Both his mother and father came out to greet them.

"Don't worry, Jonathon," his mother said. "Your great-grandmother told us where you were. She assured us you'd be back today and that you'd be fine. Hello. You must be Rebecca."

Rebecca and Jonathon exchanged glances. What was going on? How did his great-grandmother know all this?

But dinner soon banished all their unanswered questions to the backs of their minds. They had a supper of fresh vegetables, which were cooked in a tomato sauce and served over homemade pasta. For dessert there was fruit salad with vanilla ice cream. The food tasted wonderful, but like nothing Rebecca had ever experienced, especially the dessert. Blackberries, strawberries, raspberries—she felt she had never really tasted any of them before. The flavour seemed to explode in her mouth with every bite, and she sighed and exclaimed until Jonathon began to roll his eyes.

"I can't help it," she protested. "It's too delicious. Even the ice cream doesn't taste like the ice cream at home."

"Of course," Jonathon's mother said, smiling. "The fruit you're eating was picked yesterday, and there are no chemicals in our food. What you're tasting is food in its natural, fresh state."

"Amazing," sighed Rebecca. "Thank you for the meal. It was wonderful. I even liked the vegetables."

"Sorry I'm late!" a voice rang out from the front hall. Moments later, Tara came into the dining area, her cheeks flushed with excitement.

Tara, thought Rebecca. She couldn't stop staring at her as Jonathan looked after the introductions. Could this be the same Tara who had been so miserable in the future of Zanu? How happy and healthy she looked here!

Rebecca could hardly focus on the conversation—it was just too strange. Apparently, Tara had been tied up with her research at the marine zoo because they were getting close to a breakthrough—soon they expected to be able to crack the code of communication between whales. Imagine—being able to actually talk to whales! No wonder Tara was so excited.

Once dinner was finished, Jonathan's mom had her settled in the guest room, even offering her a book to read, and soon, despite the excitement—or maybe because of it—Rebecca dropped off to sleep, the book still open.

CHAPTER THIRTY-FIVE

Rebecca and Jonathon were sitting in Jonathan's literature class. The class of twelve was discussing the book Jonathon's mom had given Rebecca to read last night called *Levity*. Rebecca couldn't understand what they had found interesting about it. Everyone except her seemed to like it. She didn't know how Jonathon felt about it; he wasn't participating.

She was sitting next to him in the circle of air chairs. They were in a small cozy room, the outer wall of which was clear, looking out to a garden, the inner walls lined with holograms, mostly of wildflowers. The room was painted a pale green and the carpet was of the same colour.

She nudged Jonathon. "Did you like that book?" she whispered.

"Not really," he murmured.

"Then why not say so?"

He shrugged.

She waited for a lull in the conversation.

"I found the book really boring." There, she'd said it. "I mean, compared to, say, *The Lord of the Rings*, nothing happens in this book."

The teacher was a tall blond young man. He looked at Rebecca with a warm, tolerant smile.

"Young lady, you are a visitor here. Of course we are interested in your opinions. But we don't know the book that you are referring to."

"You *what*?" Rebecca exclaimed. "Well, how about *The Prince and the Pauper* by Mark Twain or—or—*The Owl Service* by Allan Garner or..."

"We study no authors from before zero N.E." said the teacher. "After all, we started a new calendar with our new world. N.E. stands for New Era. Explain why we shun everything before that time, Jonathan."

"Actually," Jonathon answered, his head down, "I'm not sure why."

"Jonathon," said the teacher gently, "I'm afraid you are individualizing."

"Well," Jonathon said, his voice getting stronger, "I can't explain it to Rebecca because I don't understand it myself. I think that a good book is a good book. I know those books have lots of conflict and bad things in them. But I don't see that reading that stuff will make us behave that way."

"Of course it won't, Jonathon," said the teacher, patiently. "And if you want to read those books, you go right ahead. It's just that we're not interested in discussing them with you. And that's our right, isn't it? Am I correct, class?"

The other kids nodded and murmured in agreement.

The teacher placed a hand on Jonathon's shoulder. "This is not a punishment," he said, his eyes earnest and concerned. "We only want the best for you and for ourselves. The class wants to discuss the book *Levity*. You wish to discuss books that are of no interest to us. It's only fair of you to let us continue our discussion. Does one person have the right to disrupt everyone?" He shook his head, smiled at Jonathon, and then turned his attention back to the class.

And then, as Rebecca watched, a strange thing happened. Jonathon began to speak again, but no one heard him. They talked right over him and behaved just as if he weren't there, as if he were invisible.

Rebecca stood up.

"This is terrible!" she objected in a loud voice. "You're being terribly rude. He has a right to express his opinion."

"And we, my dear," said the teacher to her with a smile, "have a right not to be bothered by such disruptions."

"Jonathon has some good ideas," Rebecca exclaimed. "What are you so afraid of?"

But no one listened to her either. She looked at Jonathon, as the class continued on around them.

"Are you just going to take this?" she said to him.

"And what would you suggest?" Jonathon replied.

"Fight. Fight them!"

"Why?"

She turned away from him and back to the teacher.

"Look here," she yelled. "I demand to be heard. My opinion is worth just as much as yours. You can't just shut people out. You might be shutting out some good ideas!" No reaction. They continued to talk quietly amongst themselves.

Rebecca was getting angrier and angrier. What could she do to get their attention?

Jonathon had a hand on her shoulder. "Calm down, Rebecca," he said. "There's nothing we can do. And if you do what you look like you're thinking of doing, you'll end up in the hospital. Violence is considered a disease here."

"I wasn't thinking of doing anything violent!" Rebecca objected. Although she had to admit to herself that the thought of a quick kick to the shins of someone, anyone, had flashed through her mind. "You mean they'd put me in the hospital," she said, full of indignation, "against my will?"

"No, if you lived here, you'd put yourself in the hospital. No-one is forced to do anything here. But you would realize how horribly sick you were and you'd go to the hospital and admit yourself for treatment."

"Just a minute," she said to Jonathon. She placed herself right in front of the teacher. She was so angry by now she felt she was about to explode.

"My name is Rebecca Lepidus. In case you don't know it, I'm from the past. I came in your time machine. I helped make this world you live in. You should learn about your history. You should read old books."

The teacher stepped around Rebecca and said in a calm, clear voice, "It is much too difficult to carry on a conversation at this moment. I suggest we all do our mathematics at our terminals and we will have the literature class later."

In a moment, everyone except Jonathon had left the room and Rebecca was left sputtering to the air.

She had never felt so frustrated. And she felt something else—she felt almost sick. It was as if her world, everything from it—the good along with the bad—was now dead. Had never been. It was like she had never been. Wiped out. Is this what she was supposed to go back and work so hard for?

"I can't believe it," she declared, turning to Jonathon. "I just can't believe it."

"Why did you get so upset?" Jonathon asked.

"Well, they just ignored us. Both of us! Didn't it bother you?"

Jonathon paused to think. "I don't know. I'm so used to it. There are certain things that everyone just accepts here. My great-grandmother gave me all of those books you were talking about. And you're right. I thought they were great. But I also found them sort of disgusting. Full of violence. And I don't dare tell anyone but her I'm reading them."

"It's strange," remarked Rebecca, taking a deep breath, trying to cool off. "You have a wonderful world here. Almost perfect. Almost. But you can't even see what's wrong with it. You're too close to it."

Jonathon stared at her.

"I guess you're right. I guess when you're inside something, so worried about what everyone will think about you, you can't really see clearly. I just figured they were right and I must be wrong to want to be different and read different things."

"It shouldn't be wrong to be different," Rebecca stated. "That much I know."

"I think," said Jonathon, "it's time for a visit to great-grandmother. We've got to get some answers."

CHAPTER THIRTY-SIX

Rebecca and Jonathon were sitting in Jonathon's great-grandmother's home later that afternoon, except his great-grandmother wasn't there yet. Rebecca was lost in thought, going over and over the scene in Jonathan's literature class.

No one had fought with her. No one had even acknowledged her opinions so they could have a good discussion. She'd just been ignored. And they were all so used to behaving this way that they couldn't see that it was—what was it, actually? Well, a sort of bullying. You weren't allowed to get out of line.

Rebecca was deflated and disappointed. She had been so happy here at first. She had thought that she'd helped to make a truly perfect world. Now she saw that it wasn't so. Although, she admitted, it was closer to perfect than her world was. Much closer.

The outer door slid up, interrupting her train of thought.

"We've come for some answers!" Jonathan declared without even saying hello. His great-grandmother walked slowly into the room. She took his hands in hers and smiled at him. Then she smiled at Rebecca.

A shock ran through Rebecca's body. Rebecca tried to smile back, but found she couldn't. She was staring at Jonathon's great-grandmother, transfixed. There was something terribly familiar about her.

"Hello, Rebecca. Hello, Jonathon. I see everything worked out all right."

Rebecca tried to swallow. She couldn't. That voice. She knew that voice. Rebecca tried to speak. Nothing came out.

The old woman sat down in a chair across from Rebecca. She sat Jonathon down beside her.

"Yes, Rebecca," the old woman said, her voice gentle, "it's me." Then she laughed, her eyes sparkling. "Or should I say you?"

Jonathon gasped. He opened and closed his mouth like a fish. His great-grandmother took his hands in hers again.

"I'm sorry, dear," she said. "It had to be this way. I couldn't tell you."

"But—it can't be," Jonathon stammered. "It can't! Why," he protested, "your name isn't Rebecca!"

"What is my name?" she asked.

"It's—oh, no—it's Beka."

"That's right, dear. Beka. And Lepidus is still my middle name."

Rebecca had been silent all this time, unable to move or talk.

Finally she spoke. "If it's true," she croaked, "then why aren't we making each other sick?"

"Perhaps," Beka answered, "because we're two very different Rebeccas. When we were split we were still practically identical. I've lived a long time since then. I've changed. I'm a different person than I was that long ago."

"But," demanded Jonathon, his face flushed, "why couldn't you tell me? You knew all along why I was having those rotten dreams!"

"I couldn't make you do anything," Jonathon's great-grandmother said, patting his cheek with her hand. "Would you have believed me had I told you the truth?"

Jonathon had to shake his head no.

"Exactly. All I could do was point you in the right direction. I couldn't fix anything or make anything happen."

"But," said Jonathon, "why did I have those dreams?"

"That," Beka replied, "is something I've never quite understood. Perhaps they were memories I passed down to you, something you inherited from me. Instead of my brown eyes," she said, looking into his green ones, "you got my memories. Or perhaps it was some sort of psychic connection. I don't know."

She turned back to Rebecca.

"I know what you want to ask me," Beka sighed, "and I wish I could answer you. But I can't."

"What? What was I going to ask?" Rebecca challenged her.

"What I did with my life—when I returned to my present."

Finally Rebecca smiled. "Right. I guess you know yourself—ourselves, us—pretty well."

"Pretty well," replied Beka with a small laugh.

"But why can't you answer me?" Rebecca protested. "I think you should. I want to know. I want to know if you're happy. And if you are, I want you to tell me all the right choices you made so I can make those and all the wrong choices you made so I won't make those."

Beka shook her head. "I can't do that."

"Why?"

"Because if I did you'd have no free choice at all. Tell me," she said very seriously, "what do you think of our world here?"

"Well," Rebecca said, "you must know what I think. I thought everything was just great until we went to school and I saw how everyone is expected to think and behave the same way. I mean, they aren't punished if they don't, but it's even worse than being punished. They get left out. No one likes to be left out."

Beka nodded. "Yes. Yes. That's it. And why are you here, now?"

Rebecca stopped to think. "Because I didn't listen to Jonathon and let myself disappear. Because I listened to myself."

Beka's face broke out into a big smile.

"Because you weren't following anyone's directions—not Jonathon's, not Lewis's and not Catherine's. And that's why you'd hate it if I told you what was going to happen, what you had to do. You'd feel like you had to do everything a certain way. You'd lose all your freedom. And things change. Who knows if your future will be this one exactly? After all, do you remember me from the time of Zanu?"

"No."

"Or from the future after a nuclear war?"

"No."

"So you see, this is just one possible timeline."

"But," Rebecca objected, "I like this one the best! I want to get to *this* one!" Then she remembered the classroom. "At least, I think I do. Do you like living here?" she asked. "Doesn't it bug you, having to be the same as everyone else? Do they tell you you're 'individualizing'?"

Beka laughed. "Yes, they do. What they don't understand is that what makes me 'individualize' is what made their world possible. We fought against the way people expected us to be—

we changed the world to this. Our ability to fight—something they feel they've grown beyond—made this all possible. On the other hand, I'd hate to lose the thing that makes this time so wonderful—the fact that everyone feels we are in this together, as equals, and that together we do well or together we tear things down." She paused. "Jonathon, you and I have some work to do still. We need to show people that they are getting too rigid and too complacent."

Jonathon grinned. "I'm ready!"

"It's amazing," Beka said, "how quickly everything did change. Just think how different Winnipeg was from 1900 to 2000—and I've seen even greater changes. And I must say, most of them are for the best."

"Most of them," Rebecca agreed. "But you know, it's nice to realize that in the future I won't be bored to death in a perfect world. There'll still be a few things for me to work on—with my great-grandson." At that she looked at Jonathon and burst out laughing.

He looked at her and turned all red.

"Yes," Rebecca laughed, "I'm your great-grandmother."

This thought struck her as so funny that she had to hold her stomach, she was laughing so hard.

'It's time," said Beka, over Rebecca's laughter, "for your trip home."

As she said that she slipped an envelope into Rebecca's hand. "Open it when you get home," she said.

* * *

Rebecca sat on the ground, in Assiniboine Park. As soon as she had arrived she'd asked a kid on his bike the date. She was back only minutes after she had left. No one would be worried about her yet. She had a few minutes to sit here quietly and to absorb everything. If she ever could. She wondered if she should tell Lewis and Catherine and Lonney where she had gone and what she had seen. She thought perhaps she had better. It would give them all hope that they could change things for the better.

She looked at the envelope she still had clutched in her hand and wasted no time tearing it open. There were two sheets of paper, very official-looking with stamps and government headings. Birth certificates! One for Catherine Lepidus. One for Lewis Lepidus. She smiled. I think of everything, she thought. Now Mom and Dad will have much less trouble adopting them.

She thought about Lewis and Catherine, then, and how she'd resented them for being so perfect. She wasn't perfect and she knew it. She also knew that she, just the way she was, could help change the world into a better place, even though it, too, might never be perfect.

And that would have to be good enough.